FIVE ON
KIRRIN
ISLAND
AGAIN

Enid Blyton's

FIVE ON KIRRIN ISLAND AGAIN

ILLUSTRATED BY JOLYNE KNOX

AWARD PUBLICATIONS

ISBN 0-86163-683-X

First published 1947 by Hodder and Stoughton Ltd
This edition 1980

This edition first published 1993 by Award Publications Limited,
1st Floor, 27 Longford Street, London NW1 3DZ

Printed in Great Britain by
Caledonian International Book Manufacturing, Glasgow

CONTENTS

1

A letter for George

Anne was trying to do some of her prep in a corner of the common-room when her cousin George came bursting in.

George was not a boy; she was a girl called Georgina, but because she had always wanted to be a boy she insisted on being called George. So George she was. She wore her curly hair cut short, and her bright blue eyes gleamed angrily now as she came towards Anne.

'Anne! I've just had a letter from home – and what do you think? Father wants to go and live on my island to do some special work – and he wants to build a sort of tower or something in the castle yard!'

The other girls looked up in amusement, and Anne held out her hand for the letter that George was waving at her. Everyone knew about the little island off Kirrin Bay that belonged to George. Kirrin Island was a tiny place with an old ruined castle in the middle of it: the home of rabbits and gulls and jackdaws.

It had underground dungeons in which George and her cousins had had one or two amazing adventures. It had

1

once belonged to George's mother, and she had given it to George – and George was very fierce where her precious Kirrin Island was concerned! It was *hers*. Nobody else must live there, or even land there without her permission.

And now, dear me, here was her father proposing to go to her island, and even build some sort of workshop there! George was red with exasperation.

'It's just like grown-ups; they go and give you things and then act as though the things were theirs all the time. I don't *want* Father living on my island, and building nasty messy sheds and things there.'

'Oh George – you know your father is a very famous scientist, who needs to work in peace,' said Anne, taking the letter. 'Surely you can lend him your island for a bit?'

'There are plenty of other places where he can work in peace,' said George. 'Oh dear – I was so hoping we could go and stay there in the Easter hols – take our boat there, and food and everything, just like we've done before. Now we shan't be able to if Father really does go there.'

Anne read the letter. It was from George's mother.

'My darling George,

'I think I must tell you at once that your father proposes to live on Kirrin Island for some little time in order to finish some very important experiments he is making. He will have to have some kind of building erected there – a sort of tower, I believe. Apparently he needs a place where he can have absolute peace and isolation, and also, for some reason, where there is water all around him. The fact of being surrounded by water is necessary to his experiment.

'Now, dear, don't be upset about this. I know that you consider Kirrin Island is your very own, but you must allow your family to share it, especially when it is for something as important as your father's scientific work. Father thinks you will be very pleased indeed to lend him Kirrin Island, but I know your funny feelings about it, so I thought I had better write and tell you, before you arrive home and see him installed there, complete with his tower.'

2

The letter then went on about other things, but Anne did not bother to read these. She looked at George.

'Oh, George! I don't see why you mind your father borrowing Kirrin Island for a bit! I wouldn't mind *my* father borrowing an island from me – if I was lucky enough to have one!'

'*Your* father would talk to you about it first, and ask your permission, and see if you minded,' said George, sulkily. 'My father never does anything like that. He just does exactly as he likes without asking anybody anything. I really do think he might have written to me himself. He just puts my back up.'

'You've got a back that is very easily put up, George,' said Anne, laughing. 'Don't scowl at me like that. *I'm* not borrowing your island without your gracious permission.'

But George wouldn't smile back. She took her letter and read it again gloomily. 'To think that all my lovely holiday plans are spoilt!' she said. 'You know how super Kirrin Island is at Easter time – all primroses and gorse and baby rabbits. And you and Julian and Dick were coming to stay, and we haven't stayed together since last summer when we went caravanning.'

'I know. It *is* hard luck!' said Anne. 'It would have been wizard to go and stay on the island these hols. But perhaps your father wouldn't mind if we did? We needn't disturb him.'

'As if living on Kirrin Island with Father there would be the same as living there all by ourselves,' said George, scornfully. 'You know it would be horrid.'

Well yes – Anne didn't think on the whole that Kirrin Island would be much fun with Uncle Quentin there. George's father was such a hot-tempered, impatient man, and when he was in the middle of one of his experiments he was quite unbearable. The least noise upset him.

'Oh dear – how he will yell at the jackdaws to keep quiet, and shout at the noisy gulls!' said Anne, beginning to giggle. 'He won't find Kirrin quite so peaceful as he imagines!'

George gave a watery sort of smile. She folded up the letter and turned away. 'Well, I think it's just the limit,' she said. 'I wouldn't have felt so bad if only Father had asked my permission.'

'He'd never do that!' said Anne. 'It just wouldn't occur to him. Now George, don't spend the rest of the day brooding over your wrongs, for goodness' sake. Go down to the kennels and fetch Timmy. He'll soon cheer you up.'

Timothy was George's dog, whom she loved with all her heart. He was a big black and white mongrel dog, with a ridiculously long tail, and a wide mouth that really seemed to smile. All the four cousins loved him. He was so friendly and loving, so lively and amusing, and he had shared so very many adventures with them all. The five of them had had many happy times together.

George went to get Timmy. Her school allowed the children to keep their own pets. If it hadn't allowed this, it is quite certain that George would not have gone to boarding-school! She could not bear to be parted from Timmy for even a day.

Timmy began to bark excitedly as soon as she came near. George lost her sulky look and smiled. Dear Timmy, dear trustable Timmy – he was better than any person! He was always on her side, always her friend whatever she did, and to Timmy there was no one in the world so wonderful as George.

They were soon going through the fields together, and George talked to Timmy as she always did. She told him about her father borrowing Kirrin Island. Timmy agreed with every word she said. He listened as if he understood everything, and not even when a rabbit shot across his path did he leave his mistress's side. Timmy always knew when George was upset.

He gave her hand a few little licks every now and again.

By the time that George was back at school again she felt much better. She took Timmy into school with her smuggling him in at a side door. Dogs were not allowed in the school building, but George, like her father, often did exactly as she liked.

She hurried Timmy up to her dormitory. He scuttled under her bed quickly and lay down. His tail thumped the floor gently. He knew what this meant. George wanted the comfort of his nearness that night! He would be able to jump on her bed, when lights were out, and snuggle into the crook of her knees. His brown eyes gleamed with delight.

'Now, lie quiet,' said George, and went out of the room to join the other girls. She found Anne, who was busy writing a letter to her brothers, Julian and Dick, at their boarding-school.

'I've told them about Kirrin Island, and your father wanting to borrow it,' she said. 'Would you like to come and stay with *us*, George, these hols, instead of us coming to Kirrin? Then you won't feel cross all the time because your father is on your island.'

'No thanks,' said George, at once. 'I'm going home. I want to keep an eye on Father! I don't want him blowing up Kirrin Island with one of his experiments. You know he's messing about with explosives now, don't you?'

'Ooooh – atom bombs, or things like that?' said Anne.

'I don't know,' said George. 'Anyway, quite apart from keeping an eye on Father and my island, we ought to go and stay at Kirrin to keep Mother company. She'll be all alone if Father's on the island. I suppose he'll take food and everything there.'

'Well, there's one thing, we shan't have to creep about on tiptoe and whisper, if your father isn't at Kirrin Cottage!' said Anne. 'We can be as noisy as we like. Do cheer up, George!'

But it took George quite a long time to get over the fit of gloom caused by her mother's letter. Even having Timmy on her bed each night, till he was discovered by an angry teacher, did not quite make up for her disappointment.

The term ran swiftly on to its end. April came in, with sunshine and showers. Holidays came nearer and nearer! Anne thought joyfully of Kirrin, with its lovely sandy beach, its blue sea, its fishing-boats and its lovely cliffside walks.

Julian and Dick thought longingly of them too. This term both they and the girls broke up on the same day.

They could meet in London and travel down to Kirrin together. Hurrah!

The day came at last. Trunks were piled in the hall. Cars arrived to fetch some of the children who lived fairly near. The school coaches drew up to take the others down to the station. There was a terrific noise of yelling and shouting everywhere. The teachers could not make themselves heard in the din.

'Anyone would think that every single child had gone completely mad,' said one of them to another. 'Oh, thank goodness, they're getting into the coaches. George! *Must* you rush along the corridor at sixty miles an hour, with Timmy barking his head off all the time!'

'Yes, I must, I must!' cried George. 'Anne, where are you? Do come and get into the coach. I've got Timmy. He knows it's holidays now. Come on, Tim!'

Down to the station went the singing crowd of children. They piled into the train. 'Bags I this seat! Who's taken my bag? Get out, Hetty, you know you can't bring your dog in here with mine. They fight like anything. Hurrah, the guard's blowing his whistle! We're off!'

The engine pulled slowly out of the station, its long train of carriages behind it, filled to bursting with girls off for their holidays. Through the quiet countryside it went, through small towns and villages, and at last ran through the smoky outskirts of London.

'The boys' train is due in two minutes before ours,' said Anne, leaning out of the window, as the train drew slowly into the London station. 'If it was punctual, they might be on our platform to meet us. Oh look, George, look – there they are!'

George hung out of the window too. 'Hi, Julian!' she yelled. 'Here we are! Hi, Dick, Julian!'

2

Back at Kirrin Cottage

Julian, Dick, Anne, George and Timmy went straight-away to have buns and ginger-beer at the station tearoom. It was good to be all together again. Timmy went nearly mad with joy at seeing the two boys. He kept trying to get on to their knees.

'Look here, Timmy, old thing, I love you very much and I'm jolly glad to see you,' said Dick, 'but that's twice you've upset my ginger-beer all over me. Has he behaved himself this term, George?'

'Fairly well,' said George, considering. 'Hasn't he, Anne? I mean – he only got the joint out of the larder once – and he didn't do so *much* harm to that cushion he chewed – and if people *will* leave their goloshes all over the place nobody can blame Timmy for having a good old game with them.'

'And that was the end of the goloshes, I suppose,' said Julian, with a grin. 'On the whole, Timmy, you have a rather poor report. I'm afraid our Uncle Quentin will not award you the usual twenty-five pence we get for good reports.'

At the mention of her father, George scowled. 'I see George has not lost her pretty scowl,' said Dick, in a teasing voice. 'Dear old George! We shouldn't know her unless she put on that fearsome scowl half a dozen times a day!'

'Oh, she's better than she was,' said Anne hurrying to George's defence at once. George was not so touchy as she had once been, when she was being teased. All the same, Anne knew that there might be sparks flying over her father taking Kirrin Island these holidays, and she didn't want George to fly into a temper too soon!

Julian looked at his cousin. 'I say, old thing, you're not going to take this business of Kirrin Island too much to heart, are you?' he said. 'You've just got to realise that your father's a remarkably clever man, one of the finest scientists we've got – and *I* think that those kind of fellows ought to be allowed as much freedom as they like, for their work. I mean – if Uncle Quentin wants to work on Kirrin Island for some peculiar reason of his own, then you ought to be pleased to say "Go ahead, Father!" '

George looked a little mutinous after this rather long speech; but she thought a great deal of Julian, and usually went by what he said. He was older than any of them, a tall, good-looking boy, with determined eyes and a strong chin. George scratched Timmy's head, and spoke in a low voice.

'All right. I won't go up in smoke about it, Julian. But I'm frightfully disappointed. I'd planned to go to Kirrin Island ourselves these hols.'

'Well, we're all disappointed,' said Julian. 'Buck up with your bun, old thing. We've got to get across London and catch the train for Kirrin. We shall miss it if we don't look out.'

Soon they were in the train for Kirrin. Julian was very

good at getting porters and taxis. Anne gazed admiringly at her big brother as he found them all corner-seats in a carriage. Julian did know how to tackle things!

'Do you think I've grown, Julian?' she asked him. 'I did hope I'd be as tall as George by the end of this term, but she grew too!'

'Well, I should think you might be a quarter of an inch taller than last term,' said Julian. 'You can't catch us up, Anne – you'll always be the smallest! But I like you small.'

'Look at Timmy, putting his head out of the window as usual!' said Dick. 'Timmy you'll get a grit in your eye. Then George will go quite mad with grief and think you're going blind!'

'Woof,' said Timmy, and wagged his tail. That was the nice part about Timmy. He always knew when he was being spoken to, even if his name was not mentioned, and he answered at once.

Aunt Fanny was at the station to meet them in the pony-trap. The children flung themselves on her, for they were very fond of her. She was kind and gentle, and did her best to keep her clever, impatient husband from finding too much fault with the children.

'How's Uncle Quentin?' asked Julian, politely, when they were setting off in the trap.

'He's very well,' said his aunt. 'And terribly excited. Really, I've never known him to be so thrilled as he has been lately. His work has been coming along very successfully.'

'I suppose you don't know what his latest experiment is?' said Dick.

'Oh no. He never tells me a word,' said Aunt Fanny. 'He never tells anyone anything while he is at work, except his colleagues, of course. But I do know it's very important – and I know, of course, that the last part of the experiment has to be made in a place where there is deep water all round. Don't ask me why! I don't know.'

'Look! There's Kirrin Island!' said Anne, suddenly. They had rounded a corner, and had come in sight of the bay. Guarding the entrance to it was the curious little island topped by the old ruined castle. The sun shone down on the blue sea, and the island looked most enchanting.

George looked earnestly at it. She was looking for the building, whatever it was, that her father said he needed for his work. Everyone looked at the island, seeking the same thing.

They saw it easily enough! Rising from the centre of the castle, probably from the castle yard, was a tall thin tower, rather like a lighthouse. At the top was a glass-enclosed room, which glittered in the sun.

'Oh Mother! I don't like it! It spoils Kirrin Island,' said George, in dismay.

'Darling, it can come down when your father has finished his work,' said her mother. 'It's a very flimsy, temporary thing. It can easily be pulled down. Father promised me he would scrap it as soon as his work was done. He says you can go across and see it, if you like. It's really rather interesting.'

'Ooooh – I'd *love* to go and see it,' said Anne, at once. 'It looks so queer. Is Uncle Quentin all alone on Kirrin Island, Aunt Fanny?'

'Yes, I don't like him to be alone,' said her aunt. 'For one thing I am sure he doesn't get his meals properly, and for another, I'm always afraid some harm might come to him when he's experimenting – and if he's alone, how would I know if anything happened to him?'

'Well, Aunt Fanny, you could always arrange for him to signal to you each morning and night, couldn't you?' said Julian, sensibly. 'He could use that tower easily. He could flash a signal to you in the morning, using a mirror, you know – heliographing that he was all right – and at night he could signal with a lamp. Easy!'

'Yes. I did suggest that sort of thing,' said his aunt. 'I said I'd go over with you all tomorrow, to see him and perhaps, Julian dear, you could arrange something of the sort with your uncle? He seems to listen to you now.'

'Gracious! Do you mean to say Father wants us to invade his secret lair, and actually to see his strange tower?' asked George, surprised. 'Well – I don't think I want to go. After all, it's *my* island – and it's horrid to see someone else taking possession of it.'

'Oh, George, don't begin all that again,' said Anne, with a sigh. 'You and your island! Can't you even *lend* it to your own father! Aunt Fanny, you should have seen George when your letter came. She looked so fierce that I was quite scared!'

Everyone laughed except George and Aunt Fanny. She looked distressed. George was always so difficult! She found fault with her father, and got up against him time after time – but dear me, how very, very like him she was, with her scowls, her sudden temper, and her fierceness! If only George was as sweet-tempered and as easy-going as these three cousins of hers!

George looked at her mother's troubled face, and felt ashamed of herself. She put her hand on her knee. 'It's all right Mother! I won't make a fuss. I'll try and keep my feelings to myself, really I will. I know Father's work is important. I'll go with you to the island tomorrow.'

Julian gave George a gentle clap on the back. 'Good old George! She's actually learned, not only to give in, but to give in gracefully! George, you're more like a boy than ever when you act like that.'

George glowed. She liked Julian to say she was like a boy. She didn't want to be petty and catty and bear malice as so many girls did. But Anne looked a little indignant.

'It isn't *only* boys that can learn to give in decently, and things like that,' she said. 'Heaps of girls do. Well, I jolly well hope I do myself!'

'My goodness, here's another fire-brand!' said Aunt Fanny, smiling. 'Stop arguing now, all of you – here's Kirrin Cottage. Doesn't it look sweet with all the primroses in the garden, and the wallflowers coming out, and the daffodils peeping everywhere?'

It certainly did. The four children and Timmy tore in at the front gate, delighted to be back. They clattered into the house, and, to their great delight, found Joanna, the old cook there. She had come back to help for the holidays. She beamed at the children, and fondled Timmy when he leapt round her barking.

'Well, there now! Haven't you all grown again? How big you are, Master Julian – taller than I am, I declare. And little Miss Anne, why, she's getting quite big.'

That pleased Anne, of course. Julian went back to the front door to help his aunt with the small bags in the trap.

The trunks were coming later. Julian and Dick took everything upstairs.

Anne joined them, eager to see her old bedroom again. Oh, how good it was to be in Kirrin Cottage once more! She looked out of the windows. One looked on to the moor at the back. The other looked sideways on to the sea. Lovely! Lovely! She began to sing a little song as she undid her bag.

'You know,' she said to Dick, when he brought George's bag in, 'you know, Dick, I'm really quite pleased that Uncle Quentin has gone to Kirrin Island, even if it means we won't be able to go there much! I feel much freer in the house when he's away. He's a very clever man and he can be awfully nice – but I always feel a bit afraid of him.'

Dick laughed. 'I'm not afraid of him – but he's a bit of a wet blanket in a house, I must say, when we're here for the holidays. Funny to think of him on Kirrin Island all alone.'

A voice came up the stairs. 'Come down to tea, children, because there are hot scones for you, just out of the oven.'

'Coming, Aunt Fanny!' called Dick. 'Hurry, Anne. I'm awfully hungry. Julian, did you hear Aunt Fanny calling?'

George came up the stairs to fetch Anne. She was pleased to be home, and as for Timmy, he was engaged in going round every single corner of the house, sniffing vigorously.

'He always does that!' said George. 'As if he thought that there *might* be a chair or a table that didn't smell quite the same as it always did. Come on, Tim. Teatime! Mother, as Father isn't here, can Timmy sit beside me on the floor? He's awfully well-behaved now.'

'Very well,' said her mother, and tea began. What a tea! It looked as if it was a spread for a party of twenty. Good old Joanna! She must have baked all day. Well, there wouldn't be much left when the Five had finished!

3

Off to Kirrin Island

Next day was fine and warm. 'We can go across to the island this morning,' said Aunt Fanny. 'We'll take our own food, because I'm sure Uncle Quentin will have forgotten we're coming.'

'Has he a boat there?' asked George. 'Mother – he hasn't taken *my* boat, has he?'

'No, dear,' said her mother. 'He's got another boat. I was afraid he would never be able to get it in and out of all those dangerous rocks round the island, but he got one of the fishermen to take him, and had his own boat towed behind, with all its stuff in.'

'Who built the tower?' asked Julian.

'Oh, he made out the plans himself and some men were sent down from the Ministry of Research to put the tower up for him,' said Aunt Fanny. 'It was all rather hush-hush really. The people here were most curious about it, but they don't know any more than I do! No local man helped in the building, but one or two fishermen were hired to

15

take the material to the island, and to land the men and so on.'

'It's all very mysterious,' said Julian. 'Uncle Quentin leads rather an exciting life, really, doesn't he? I wouldn't mind being a scientist myself. I want to be something really worthwhile when I grown up – I'm not just going into somebody's office. I'm going to be on my own.'

'I think I shall be a doctor,' said Dick.

'I'm off to get my boat,' said George, rather bored with this talk. She knew what *she* was going to do when she was grown-up – live on Kirrin Island with Timmy!

Aunt Fanny had got ready plenty of food to take across to the island. She was quite looking forward to the trip. She had not seen her husband for some days, and was anxious to know that he was all right.

They all went down to the beach, Julian carrying the bag of food. George was already there with her boat. James, a fisher-boy friend of George's, was there too, ready to push the boat out for them.

He grinned at the children. He knew them all well. In the old days he had looked after Timmy for George when her father had said the dog must be given away. George had never forgotten James's kindness to Timmy, and always went to see him every holidays.

'Going off to the island?' said James. 'That's a queer thing in the middle of it, isn't it? Kind of lighthouse, it looks. Take my hand, Miss, and let me help you in.'

Anne took his hand and jumped into the boat. George was already there with Timmy. Soon they were all in. Julian and George took the oars. James gave them a shove and off they went on the calm, clear water. Anne could see every stone on the bottom!

Julian and George rowed strongly. They sent the boat along swiftly. George began to sing a rowing song and they all took it up. It was lovely to be on the sea in a boat again. Oh holidays, go slowly, don't rush away too fast!

'George,' said her mother nervously, as they came near to Kirrin Island, 'you *will* be careful of these awful rocks, won't you? The water's so clear today that I can see them all – and some of them are only just below the water.'

'Oh Mother! You know I've rowed hundreds of times to Kirrin Island!' laughed George. 'I simply *couldn't* go on a rock! I know them all, really I do. I could almost row blindfold to the island now.'

There was only one place to land on the island in safety. This was a little cove, a natural little harbour running up to a stretch of sand. It was sheltered by high rocks all round. George and Julian worked their way to the east side of the island, rounded a low wall of very sharp rocks, and there lay the cove, a smooth inlet of water running into the shore!

Anne had been looking at the island as the others rowed. There was the old ruined Kirrin Castle in the centre, just the same as ever. Its tumbledown towers were full of jackdaws as usual. Its old walls were gripped by ivy.

'It's a lovely place!' said Anne, with a sigh. Then she gazed at the curious tower that now rose from the centre of the castle yard. It was not built of brick but some smooth, shiny material, that was fitted together in sections. Evidently the tower had been made in that way so that it might be brought to the island easily, and set up there quickly.

'Isn't it queer?' said Dick. 'Look at that little glass room at the top – like a look-out room! I wonder what it's for?'

'Can anyone climb up inside the tower?' asked Dick, turning to Aunt Fanny.

'Oh yes. There is a narrow spiral staircase inside,' said his aunt. 'That's about all there is inside the tower itself. It's the little room at the top that is important. It has got some extraordinary wiring there, essential to your uncle's experiments. I don't think he *does* anything with the tower – it just has to be there, doing something on its own, which has a certain effect on the experiments he is making.'

Anne couldn't follow this. It sounded too complicated. 'I should like to go up the tower,' she said.

'Well, perhaps your uncle will let you,' said her aunt.

'If he's in a good temper,' said George.

'Now George – you're not to say things like that,' said her mother.

The boat ran into the little harbour, and grounded softly. There was another boat there already – Uncle Quentin's.

George leapt out with Julian and they pulled it up a little further, so that the others could get out without wetting their feet. Out they all got, and Timmy ran up the beach in delight.

'Now, Timmy!' said George, warningly, and Timmy turned a despairing eye on his mistress. Surely she wasn't going to stop him looking to see if there were any rabbits? Only just *looking*! What harm was there in that?

Ah – there was a rabbit! And another and another! They sat all about, looking at the little company coming

18

up from the shore. They flicked their ears and twitched their noses, keeping quite still.

'Oh, they're as tame as ever!' said Anne in delight. 'Aunty Fanny, aren't they lovely? Do look at the baby one over there. He's washing his face!'

They stopped to look at the rabbits. They really were astonishingly tame. But then very few people came to Kirrin Island, and the rabbits multiplied in peace, running about where they liked, quite unafraid.

'Oh, that one is . . .' began Dick, but then the picture was spoilt. Timmy, quite unable to do nothing but look, had suddenly lost his self-control and was bounding on the surprised rabbits. In a trice nothing could be seen but white bobtails flashing up and down as rabbit after rabbit rushed to its burrow.

'*Timmy!*' called George, crossly, and poor Timmy put his tail down, looking round at George miserably. 'What!' he seemed to say. 'Not even a scamper after the rabbits? What a hard-hearted mistress!'

'Where's Uncle Quentin?' asked Anne, as they walked to the great broken archway that was the entrance to the old castle. Behind it were the stone steps that led towards the centre. They were broken and irregular now. Aunt Fanny went across them carefully, afraid of stumbling, but the children, who were wearing rubber shoes, ran over them quickly.

They passed through an old ruined doorway into what looked like a great yard. Once there had been a stone-paved floor, but now most of it was covered by sand, and by close-growing weeds or grass.

The castle had had two towers. One was almost a complete ruin. The other was in better shape. Jackdaws circled round it, and flew above the children's heads, crying 'chack, chack, chack'.

'I suppose your father lives in the little old room with the two slit-like windows,' said Dick to George. 'That's the only place in the castle that would give him any shelter. Everywhere else is in ruins except that one room. Do you remember we once spent a night there?'

'Yes,' said George. 'It was fun. I suppose that's where Father lives. There's nowhere else – unless he's down in the dungeons!'

'Oh, no one would live in the dungeons surely, unless they simply *had* to!' said Julian. 'They're so dark and cold. Where *is* your father, George? I can't see him anywhere.'

'Mother, where would Father be?' asked George. 'Where's his workshop – in that old room there?' She pointed to the dark, stone-walled, stone-roofed room, which was really all that was left of the part in which people had long ago lived. It jutted out from what had once been the wall of the castle.

'Well, really, I don't exactly know,' said her mother. 'I suppose he works over there. He's always met me down at the cove, and we've just sat on the sand and had a picnic and talked. He didn't seem to want me to poke round much.'

'Let's call him,' said Dick. So they shouted loudly.

'Uncle QUEN-tin! Uncle QUEN-tin! Where åre you?'

The jackdaws flew up in fright, and a few gulls, who had been sitting on part of the ruined wall, joined in the noise, crying 'ee-oo, ee-oo, ee-oo' over and over again. Every rabbit disappeared in a trice.

No Uncle Quentin appeared. They shouted again.

'UNCLE QUENTIN! WHERE ARE YOU?'

'What a noise!' said Aunt Fanny, covering her ears. 'I should think that Joanna must have heard that at home. Oh dear – where is your uncle? This is most annoying of him. I *told* him I'd bring you across today.'

'Oh well – he must be somewhere about,' said Julian, cheerfully. 'If Mahomet won't come to the mountain, then the mountain must go to Mahomet. I expect he's deep in some book or other. We'll hunt for him.'

'We'll look in that little dark room,' said Anne. So they all went through the stone doorway, and found themselves in a little dark room, lit only by two slits of windows. At one end was a space, or recess, where a fireplace had once been, going back into the thick stone wall.

'He's not here,' said Julian in surprise. 'And what's more – there's nothing here at all! No food, no clothes, no books, no stores of any sort. This is not his workroom, nor even his store!'

'Then he must be down in the dungeons,' said Dick. 'Perhaps it's necessary to his work to be underground – and with water all round! Let's go and find the entrance. We know where it is – not far from the old well in the middle of the yard.'

'Yes. He must be down in the dungeons. Mustn't he, Aunt Fanny?' said Anne. 'Are you coming down?'

'Oh no,' said her aunt. 'I can't bear those dungeons. I'll sit out here in the sun, in this sheltered corner, and unpack the sandwiches. It's almost lunch-time.'

'Oh good,' said everyone. They went towards the dungeon entrance. They expected to see the big flat stone that covered the entrance, standing upright, so that they might go down the steps underground.

But the stone was lying flat. Julian was just about to pull on the iron ring to lift it up when he noticed something peculiar.

'Look,' he said. 'There are weeds growing round the edges of the stone. Nobody has lifted it for a long time. Uncle Quentin isn't down in the dungeons!'

'Then where *is* he?' said Dick. 'Wherever *can* he be?'

4

Where is Uncle Quentin?

The four of them, with Timmy nosing round their legs, stood staring down at the big stone that hid the entrance to the dungeons. Julian was perfectly right. The stone could not have been lifted for months, because weeds had grown closely round the edges, sending their small roots into every crack.

'No one is down there,' said Julian. 'We need not even bother to pull up the stone and go down to see. If it had been lifted lately, those weeds would have been torn up as it was raised.'

'And anyway, we know that no one can get *out* of the dungeon once the entrance stone is closing it,' said Dick. 'It's too heavy. Uncle Quentin wouldn't be silly enough to shut himself in! He'd leave it open.'

'Of course he would,' said Anne. 'Well – he's not there, then. He must be somewhere else.'

'But *where*?' said George. 'This is only a small island, and we know every corner of it. Oh – would he be in that cave we hid in once? The only cave on the island?'

'Oh yes – he might be,' said Julian. 'But I doubt it. I can't see Uncle Quentin dropping down through the hole in the cave's roof – and that's the only way of getting into it unless you're going to clamber and slide about the rocks on the shore for ages. I can't see him doing that, either.'

They made their way beyond the castle to the other side of the island. Here there was a cave they had once lived in. It could be entered with difficulty on the seaward side, as Julian had said, by clambering over slippery rocks, or it could be entered by dropping down a rope through a hole in the roof to the floor some way below.

They found the hole, half hidden in old heather. Julian felt about. The rope was still there. 'I'll slide down and have a look,' he said.

He went down the rope. It was knotted at intervals so that his feet found holding-places and he did not slide down too quickly and scorch his hands.

He was soon in the cave. A dim light came in from the seaward side. Julian took a quick look round. There was absolutely nothing there at all, except for an old box that they must have left behind when they were last here themselves.

He climbed up the rope again, his head appearing suddenly out of the hole. Dick gave him a hand.

'Well?' he said. 'Any sign of Uncle Quentin?'

'No,' said Julian. 'He's not there, and hasn't been there either, I should think. It's a mystery! Where is he, and if he's really doing important work where is all his stuff? I mean, we know that plenty of stuff was brought here because Aunt Fanny told us so.'

'Do you think he's in the tower?' said Anne, suddenly. 'He might be in that glass room at the top.'

'Well, he'd see us at once, if he were!' said Julian, scornfully. '*And* hear our yells too! Still, we might as well have a look.'

So back to the castle they went and walked to the queer

tower. Their aunt saw them and called to them. 'Your lunch is ready. Come and have it. Your uncle will turn up, I expect.'

'But Aunt Fanny where is he?' said Anne, with a puzzled face. 'We've looked simply *every*where!'

Her aunt did not know the island as well as the children did. She imagined that there were plenty of places to shelter in, or to work in. 'Never mind,' she said, looking quite undisturbed. 'He'll turn up later. You come along and have your meal.'

'We think we'll go up the tower,' said Julian. 'Just in case he's up there working.'

The four children and Timmy went to where the tower rose up from the castle yard. They ran their hands over the smooth, shining sections, which were fitted together in curving rows. 'What's this stuff it's built of?' said Dick.

'Some kind of new plastic material, I should think,' said Julian. 'Very light and strong, and easily put together.'

'I should be afraid it would blow down in a gale,' said George.

'Yes, so should I,' said Dick. 'Look – here is the door.'

The door was small, and rounded at the top. A key was in the keyhole. Julian turned it and unlocked the door. It opened outwards not inwards. Julian put his head inside and looked round.

There was not much room in the tower. A spiral staircase, made of the same shiny stuff as the tower itself, wound up and up and up. There was a space at one side of it, into which projected curious hook-like objects made of what looked like steel. Wire ran from one to the other.

'Better not touch them,' said Julian, looking curiously at them. 'Goodness, this is like a tower out of a fairy-tale. Come on – I'm going up the stairs to the top.'

He began to climb the steep, spiral stairway. It made him quite giddy to go up and round, up and round so many, many times.

The others followed him. Tiny, slit-like windows, set sideways not downwards, were let into the side of the tower here and there, and gave a little light to the stair-way. Julian looked through one, and had a wonderful view of the sea and the mainland.

He went on up to the top. When he got there he found himself in a small round room, whose sides were of thick, gleaming glass. Wires ran right into the glass itself, and then pierced through it, the free ends waving and glitter-ing in the strong wind that blew round the tower.

There was nothing in the little room at all! Certainly Uncle Quentin was not there. It was clearly only a tower meant to take the wires up on the hook-like things, and to run them through the strange, thick glass at the top, and set them free in the air. What for? Were they catching some kind of wireless waves? Was it to do with Radar? Julian wondered, frowning, what was the meaning of the tower and the thin, shining wires?

The others crowded into the little room. Timmy came too, having managed the spiral stairs with difficulty.

'Gracious! What a queer place!' said George. 'My goodness, what a view we've got from here. We can see miles and miles out to sea – and on this other side we can see miles and miles across the bay, over the mainland to the hills beyond.'

'Yes. It's lovely,' said Anne. 'But – *where* is Uncle Quentin? We still haven't found him. I suppose he *is* on the island.'

'Well, his boat was pulled up in the cove,' said George. 'We saw it.'

'Then he must be here somewhere,' said Dick. 'But he's not in the castle, he's not in the dungeons, he's not in the cave and he's not up here. It's a first-class mystery.'

'The Missing Uncle. Where is he?' said Julian. 'Look there's poor Aunt Fanny still down there, waiting with the lunch. We'd better go down. She's signalling to us.'

'I should like to,' said Anne. 'It's an awful squash in this tiny glass room. I say – did you feel the tower sway then, when that gust of wind shook it? I'm going down quickly, before the whole thing blows over!'

She began to go down the spiral stairs, holding on to a little hand-rail that ran down beside them. The stairs were so steep that she was afraid of falling. She nearly *did* fall when Timmy pushed his way past her, and disappeared below at a remarkably fast pace.

Soon they were all down at the bottom. Julian locked the door again. 'Not much good locking a door if you leave the key in,' he said. 'Still – I'd better.'

They walked over to Aunt Fanny. 'Well, I thought you were never coming!' she said. 'Did you see anything interesting up there?'

'Only a lovely view,' said Anne. 'Simply magnificent. But we didn't find Uncle Quentin. It's very mysterious, Aunt Fanny – we really have looked everywhere on the island – but he's just not here.'

'And yet his boat is in the cove,' said Dick. 'So he can't have gone.'

'Yes, it does sound queer,' said Aunt Fanny, handing round the sandwiches. 'But you don't know your uncle as well as I do. He always turns up all right. He's forgotten I was bringing you, or he would be here. As it is, we may not see him, if he's quite forgotten about your coming. If he remembers, he'll suddenly turn up.'

'But where from?' asked Dick, munching a potted meat sandwich. 'He's done a jolly good disappearing trick, Aunt Fanny.'

'Well, you'll see where he comes from, I've no doubt, when he arrives,' said Aunt Fanny. 'Another Sandwich George? No, *not* you, Timmy. You've had three already. Oh george, do keep Timmy's head out of that plate.'

'He's hungry too, Mother,' said George.

'Well, I've brought dog-biscuits for him,' said her mother.

'Oh, Mother! As if Timmy would eat *dog* biscuits when he can have sandwiches,' said George. 'He only eats dog biscuits when there's absolutely nothing else and he's so ravenous he can't help eating them.'

They sat in the warm April sunshine, eating hungrily. There was orangeade to drink, cool and delicious. Timmy wandered over to a rock pool he knew, where rain-water collected, and he could be heard lapping there.

'Hasn't he got a good memory?' said George proudly. 'It's ages since he was here – and yet he remembered that pool at once, when he felt thirsty.'

'It's funny Timmy hasn't found Uncle Quentin, isn't it?' said Dick, suddenly. 'I mean – when we were hunting for him, and got "Warm" you'd think Timmy would bark or scrape about or something. But he didn't.

'I think it's jolly funny that Father can't be found anywhere,' said George. 'I do really. I can't think how you can take it so calmly, Mother.'

'Well, dear, as I said before, I know your father better than you do,' said her mother. 'He'll turn up in his own good time. Why, I remember once when he was doing some sort of work in the stalactite caves at Cheddar, he disappeared in them for over a week – but he wandered out all right when he had finished his experiments.'

'It's very queer,' began Anne, and then stopped suddenly. A curious noise came to their ears – a rumbling grumbling, angry noise, like a giant hidden dog, growling in fury. Then there was a hissing noise from the tower, and all the wires that waved at the top were suddenly lit up as if by lightning.

'There now – I knew your father was somewhere about,' said George's mother. 'I heard that noise when I was here before – but I couldn't make out where it came from.'

'Where *did* it come from?' said Dick. 'It sounded almost as if it was underneath us, but it couldn't have been. Gracious, this is most mysterious.'

No more noises came. They each helped themselves to buns with jam in the middle. And then Anne gave a squeal that made them all jump violently.

'Look! *There's* Uncle Quentin! Standing over there, near the tower. He's watching the jackdaws! Wherever *did* he come from?'

5

A mystery

Everyone stared at Uncle Quentin. There he was, intently watching the jackdaws, his hands in his pockets. He hadn't seen the children or his wife.

Timmy leapt to his feet, and gambolled over to George's father. He barked loudly. Uncle Quentin jumped and turned round. He saw Timmy – and then he saw all the others, staring at him in real astonishment.

Uncle Quentin did not look particularly pleased to see anyone. He walked slowly over to them, a slight frown on his face. 'This *is* a surprise,' he said. 'I had no idea you were all coming today.'

'Oh *Quentin*!' said his wife, reproachfully. 'I wrote it down for you in your diary. You know I did.'

'Did you! Well, I haven't looked at my diary since, so it's no wonder I forgot,' said Uncle Quentin, a little peevishly. He kissed his wife, George and Anne, and shook hands with the boys.

'Uncle Quentin – where did you come from?' asked Dick, who was eaten up with curiosity. 'We've looked for you for ages.'

'Oh, I was in my workroom,' said Uncle Quentin, vaguely.

'Well, but where's that?' demanded Dick. 'Honestly, Uncle, we can't imagine where you hide yourself. We even went up the tower to see if you were in that funny glass room at the top.'

'*What!*' exploded his uncle, in a sudden surprising fury. 'You dared to go up there? You might have been in great danger. I've just finished an experiment, and all those wires in there were connected with it.'

'Yes, we saw them acting a bit queerly,' said Julian.

'You've no business to come over here, and interfere with my work,' said his uncle, still looking furious. 'How did you get into that tower? I locked it.'

'Yes, it was locked all right,' said Julian. 'But you left the key in, you see, Uncle – so I thought it wouldn't matter if . . .'

'Oh, that's where the key is, is it?' said his uncle. 'I thought I'd lost it. Well, don't you ever go into that tower again. I tell you, it's dangerous.'

'Uncle Quentin, you haven't told us yet where your workroom is,' said Dick, who was quite determined to know. 'We can't imagine where you suddenly came from.'

'I told them you would turn up, Quentin,' said his wife. 'You look a bit thin, dear. Have you been having regular meals. You know, I left you plenty of good soup to heat up.'

'Did you?' said her husband. 'Well, I don't know if I've had it or not. I don't worry about meals when I'm working. I'll have some of those sandwiches now, though, if nobody else wants them.'

He began to devour the sandwiches, one after another, as if he was ravenous. Aunt Fanny watched him in distress.

'Oh Quentin – you're starving. I shall come over here and stay and look after you!'

Her husband looked alarmed. 'Oh no! Nobody is to come here. I can't have my work interfered with. I'm working on an extremely important discovery.'

'Is it a discovery that nobody else knows about?' asked Anne, her eyes wide with admiration. How clever Uncle Quentin was!

'Well – I'm not sure about that,' said Uncle Quentin, taking two sandwiches at once. 'That's partly why I came over here – besides the fact that I wanted water round me and above me. I have a feeling that somebody knows a bit more than I want them to know. But there's one thing – they can't come here unless they're shown the way through all those rocks that lie round the island. Only a few of the fishermen know that, and they've been given orders not to bring anyone here at all. I think you're the only other person that knows the way, George.'

'Uncle Quentin – please do tell us where your work-room is,' begged Dick, feeling that he could not wait a single moment more to solve the mystery.

'Don't keep bothering your uncle,' said his aunt, annoyingly. 'Let him eat his lunch. He can't have had anything for ages!'

'Yes, but Aunt Fanny, I . . .' began Dick and was interrupted by his uncle.

'You obey your aunt, young man. I don't want to be pestered by any of you. What does it matter where I work?'

'Oh, it doesn't really matter a bit, sir,' said Dick, hurriedly. 'It's only that I'm awfully curious to know. You see, we looked for you simply everywhere.'

'Well, you're not quite so clever as you thought you were then,' said Uncle Quentin, and reached for a jammy bun. 'George, take this dog of yours away from me. He keeps breathing down my neck, hoping I shall give him a tit-bit. I don't approve of tit-bits at meal-times.'

George pulled Timmy away. Her mother watched her father gobbling up the rest of the food. Most of the sandwiches she had saved for tea-time had gone already. Poor Quentin! How very hungry he must be.

'Quentin, you don't think there's any danger for you here, do you?' she said. 'I mean – you don't think anyone would try to come spying on you, as they did once before?'

'No. How could they?' said her husband. 'No plane can land on this island. No boat can get through the rocks unless the way through is known, and the sea's too rough round the rocks for any swimmer.'

'Julian, see if you can make him promise to signal to me night and morning,' said Aunt Fanny, turning to her nephew. 'I feel worried about him somehow.'

Julian tackled his uncle manfully. 'Uncle, it wouldn't be too much of a bother to you to signal to Aunt Fanny twice a day, would it?'

'If you don't, Quentin, I shall come over every single day to see you,' said his wife.

'And we might come too,' said Anne mischievously. Her uncle looked most dismayed at the idea.

'Well, I could signal in the morning and in the evening when I go up to the top of the tower,' he said, 'I have to go up once every twelve hours to re-adjust the wires. I'll signal then. Half past ten in the morning and half past ten at night.'

'How will you signal?' asked Julian. 'Will you flash with a mirror in the morning?'

'Yes – that would be quite a good idea,' said his uncle. 'I could do that easily. And I'll use a lantern at night. I'll shine it out six times at half past ten. Then perhaps you'll all know I'm all right and will leave me alone! But don't look for the signal tonight. I'll start tomorrow morning.'

'Oh Quentin dear, you do sound cross,' said his wife. 'I don't like you being all alone here, that's all. You look thin and tired. I'm sure you're not . . .'

Uncle Quentin put on a scowl exactly like George sometimes put on. He looked at his wrist-watch. 'Well I must go,' he said. 'Time to get to work again. I'll see you to your boat.'

'We're going to stay to tea here, Father,' said George.

'No, I'd rather you didn't,' said her father, getting up. 'Come on – I'll take you to your boat.'

'But Father – I haven't been on my island for ages!' said George, indignantly. 'I want to stay here a bit longer. I don't see why I shouldn't.'

'Well, I've had enough interruption to my work,' said her father. 'I want to get on.'

'We shan't disturb you, Uncle Quentin,' said Dick, who was still terribly curious to know where his uncle had his workroom. Why wouldn't he tell them! Was he just being annoying? Or didn't he want them to know?

Uncle Quentin led them all firmly towards the little cove. It was plain that he meant them to go and to go quickly.

'When shall we come over and see you again, Quentin?' asked his wife.

'Not till I say so,' said her husband. 'It won't take me long now to finish what I'm on. My word, that dog's got a rabbit at last!'

'Oh *Timmy*!' yelled George in distress. Timmy dropped the rabbit he had actually managed to grab. It scampered away unhurt. Timmy came to his mistress looking very sheepish.

'You're a very bad dog. Just because I took my eye off you for half a second! No, it's no good licking my hand like that. I'm cross.'

They all came to the boat. 'I'll push her off,' said Julian. 'Get in, all of you. Well, good-bye, Uncle Quentin. I hope your work goes well.'

Everyone got into the boat. Timmy tried to put his head on George's knee, but she pushed it away.

'Oh, be kind to him and forgive him,' begged Anne. 'He looks as if he's going to cry.'

'Are you ready?' cried Julian. 'Got the oars, George? Dick, take the other pair.'

He shoved the boat off and leapt in himself. He cupped his hands round his mouth. 'Don't forget to signal, sir! We'll be watching out morning and evening!'

'And if you forget, I shall come over the very next day!' called his wife.

The boat slid away down the little inlet of water, and Uncle Quentin was lost to sight. Then round the low wall of rocks went the boat, and was soon on the open sea.

'Ju, watch and see if you can make out where Uncle Quentin is, when we're round these rocks,' said Dick. 'See what direction he goes in.'

Julian tried to see his uncle, but the rocks just there hid the cove from sight, and there was no sign of him at all.

'*Why* didn't he want us to stay? Because he didn't want us to know his hiding-place!' said Dick. 'And *why* doesn't he want us to know? Because it's somewhere *we* don't know, either!'

'But I thought we knew every single corner of my island,' said George. 'I think it's mean of Father not to tell me, if it's somewhere I don't know. I can't think *where* it can be!'

Timmy put his head on her knee again. George was so absorbed in trying to think where her father's hiding place could be that she absent-mindedly stroked Timmy's head. He was almost beside himself with delight. He licked her fingers lovingly.

'Oh Timmy – I didn't mean to pet you for ages,' said George. 'Stop licking my hands. You make them feel wet and horrid. Dick, it's very mysterious, isn't it – where *can* Father be hiding?'

'I can't imagine,' said Dick. He looked back at the island. A cloud of jackdaws rose up into the air calling loudly, 'Chack, chack, chack!'

The boy watched them. What had disturbed them? Was it Uncle Quentin? Perhaps his hiding-place was somewhere about that old tower then, the one the jackdaws nested in? On the other hand, the jackdaws often rose into the air together for no reason at all.

'Those jackdaws are making a bit of fuss,' he said.

'Perhaps Uncle's hiding-place is not far from where they roost together, by that tower.'

'Can't be,' said Julian. 'We went all round there today.'

'Well, it's a mystery,' said George, gloomily, 'and I think it's horrible having a mystery about my very own island – and to be forbidden to go to it, and solve it. It's really *too* bad!'

6

Up on the cliff

The next day was rainy. The four children put on their macintoshes and sou'-westers and went out for a walk with Timmy. They never minded the weather. In fact Julian said that he really *liked* the feel of the wind and rain buffeting against his face.

'We forgot that Uncle Quentin couldn't flash to us if the weather wasn't sunny!' said Dick. 'Do you suppose he'll find some way to signal instead?'

'No,' said George. 'He just won't bother. He thinks we're awful fussers anyway, I'm sure. We'll have to watch at half past ten tonight to see if he signals.'

'I say! Shall I be able to stay up till then?' said Anne pleased.

'I shouldn't think so,' said Dick. 'I expect Julian and I will stay up – but you kids will have to buzz off to bed!'

George gave him a punch. 'Don't call us *"kids"*! I'm almost as tall as you are now.'

'It's not much use waiting about till half past ten now to see if Uncle signals to us in any way, is it?' said Anne. 'Let's go up on the cliff – it'll be lovely and blowy. Timmy will like that. I love to see him racing along in the wind, with his ears blown back straight!'

'Woof,' said Timmy.

'He says he likes to see you with yours blown back too,' said Julian, gravely. Anne gave a squeal of laughter.

'You really are an idiot, Ju! Come on – let's take the cliff-path!'

They went up the cliff. At the top it was very windy indeed. Anne's sou'-wester was blown to the back of her head. The rain stung their cheeks and made them gasp.

'I should think we must be about the only people out this morning!' gasped George.

'Well, you're wrong,' said Julian. 'There are two people coming towards us!'

So there was. They were a man and a boy, both well wrapped up in macintoshes and sou'-westers. Like the children, they too wore high rubber boots.

The children took a look at them as they passed. The man was tall and well built, with shaggy eyebrows and a determined mouth. The boy was about sixteen, also tall and well built. He was not a bad-looking boy, but he had rather a sullen expression.

'Good morning,' said the man, and nodded. 'Good morning,' chorused the children, politely. The man looked them over keenly, and then he and the boy went on.

'Wonder who they are?' said George. 'Mother didn't say there were any new people here.'

'Just walked over from the next village, I expect,' said Dick.

They went on for some way. 'We'll walk to the coast-guard's cottage and then go back,' said Julian. 'Hi, Tim, don't go so near the cliff!'

The coastguard lived in a little whitewashed cottage on the cliff, facing the sea. Two other cottages stood beside it, also whitewashed. The children knew the coastguard well. He was a red-faced, barrel-shaped man, fond of joking.

He was nowhere to be seen when they came to his cottage. Then they heard his enormous voice singing a sea-shanty in the little shed behind. They went to find him.

'Hallo, coastguard,' said Anne.

He looked up and grinned at the children. He was busy making something. 'Hallo to you!' he said. 'So you're back again are you? Bad pennies, the lot of you – always turning up when you're not wanted!'

'What are you making?' asked Anne.

'A windmill for my young grandson,' said the coastguard, showing it to Anne. He was very clever at making toys.

'Oh, it's *lovely*,' said Anne, taking it in her hands. 'Does the windmill part go round – oh yes – it's super, coastguard!'

'I've been making quite a bit of money out of my toys,' said the old fellow, proudly. 'I've got some new neighbours in the next cottage – man and a boy – and the man's been buying all the toys I make. Seems to have a lot of nephews and nieces! He gives me good prices too.'

'Oh – would that be the man and the boy we met, I wonder?' said Dick. 'Both tall, and well built – and the man had shaggy eyebrows.'

'That's right,' said the coastguard, trimming a bit of his windmill. 'Mr Curton and his son. They came here some weeks ago. You ought to get to know the son, Master Julian. He's about your age, I should think. Must be pretty lonely for him up here!'

'Doesn't he go to any school?' asked Julian.

'No. He's been ill, so his father said. Got to have plenty of sea-air and that sort of thing. Not a bad sort of boy. He comes and helps me with my toys sometimes. And he likes to mess about with my telescope.'

'I do too,' said George. 'I love looking through your telescope. Can I look through now? I'd like to see if I can spot Kirrin Island.'

'Well, you won't see much this weather,' said the coastguard. 'You wait a few minutes. See that break in the clouds? Well, it'll clear in a few minutes, and you'll be able to see your island easily. That's a funny thing your father's built there, Miss. Part of his work, I suppose.'

'Yes,' said George. 'Oh Timmy – look what he's done, coastguard – he's upset that tin of paint. Bad boy, Timmy!'

'It's not my tin,' said the coastguard. 'It's a tin belonging to that young fellow next door. I told you he comes in to help me sometimes. He brought in that tin to help paint a little dolls' house I made for his father.'

'Oh dear,' said George, in dismay. 'Do you think he'll be cross when he knows Timmy spilt it?'

'Shouldn't think so,' said the coastguard. 'He's a queer boy though – quiet and a bit sulky. Not a bad boy, but doesn't seem very friendly like.'

George tried to clear up the mess of paint. Timmy had some on his paws, and made a little pattern of green paw-marks as he pattered about the shed.

'I'll tell the boy I'm sorry, if I meet him on the way back,' she said. 'Timmy if you dare to go near any more tins of paint you shan't sleep on my bed tonight.'

'The weather's a bit clearer now,' said Dick. 'Can we have a squint through the telescope, coastguard?'

'Let *me* see my island first,' said George at once. She tilted the telescope in the direction of Kirrin Island. She looked through it earnestly, and a smile came over her face.

'Yes, I can see it clearly. There's the tower Father has had built. I can even see the glass room quite clearly, and there's nobody in it. No sign of Father anywhere.'

Everyone had a turn at looking through the telescope. It

was fascinating to see the island appearing so close. On a clear day it would be even easier to see all the details. 'I can see a rabbit scampering,' said Anne, when her turn came.

'Don't you let that dog of yours squint through the telescope then,' said the coastguard at once. 'He'll try to get down it after that rabbit!'

Timmy cocked his ears up at the mention of the word rabbit. He looked all round and sniffed. No, there was no rabbit. Then why did people mention them?

'We'd better go now,' said Julian. 'We'll be up here again sometime, and we'll come and see what toys you've done. Thanks for letting us look through the telescope.'

'You're welcome!' said the old fellow. 'You're not likely to wear it out through looking! Come along any time you want to use it.'

They said good-bye and went off, Timmy capering round them. 'Couldn't we see Kirrin Island well!' said Anne. 'I wished I could see where your father was, George. Wouldn't it be fun if we spotted him just coming out of his hiding-place?'

The four children had discussed this problem a good deal since they had left the island. It puzzled them very much indeed. How did it happen that George's father knew a hiding-place that they didn't know? Why, they had been over every inch of the island! It must be quite a big hiding-place too, if he had got all his stuff for his experiments with him. According to George's mother, there had been quite a lot of this, to say nothing of stores of food.

'If Father knew a place I didn't know, and never told me about it, I think he's jolly mean,' George said half a dozen times. 'I do really. It's *my* island!'

'Well, he'll probably tell you when he's finished the work he's on,' said Julian. 'Then you'll know. We can all go and explore it then, wherever it is.'

After they left the coastguard's cottage they turned their steps home. They made their way along the cliff, and then saw the boy they had met before. He was standing on the path looking out to sea. The man was not with him.

He turned as they came up and gave them a pale kind of smile. 'Hallo! Been up to see the coastguard?'

'Yes,' said Julian. 'Nice old fellow, isn't he?'

'I say,' said George, 'I'm so sorry but my dog upset a tin

of green paint, and the coastguard said it was yours. Can I pay you for it, please?'

'Goodness, no!' said the boy. 'I don't mind. There wasn't much of it left anyway. That's a nice dog of yours.'

'Yes, he is,' said George, warmly. 'Best dog in the world. I've had him for years, but he's still as young as ever. Do you like dogs?'

'Oh yes,' said the boy, but he made no move to pat Timmy or fuss him, as most people did. And Timmy did not run round the boy and sniff at him as he usually did when he met anyone new. He just stood by George, his tail neither up nor down.

'That's an interesting little island,' said the boy, pointing to Kirrin. 'I wish I could go there.'

'It's *my* island,' said George, proudly. 'My very own.'

'Really?' said the boy, politely. 'Could you let me go over one day then?'

'Well – not just at present,' said George. 'You see, my father's there – working – he's a scientist.'

'Really?' said the boy again. 'Er – has he got some new experiment on hand, then?'

'Yes,' said George.

'Ah – and that queer tower is something to do with it, I suppose,' said the boy, looking interested for the first time. 'When will his experiment be finished?'

'What's that to do with you?' said Dick, suddenly. The others stared at him in surprise. Dick sounded rather rude, and it was not like him.

'Oh nothing!' said the boy, hastily. 'I only thought that if his work will soon be finished, perhaps your brother would take me over to his island!'

George couldn't help feeling pleased. This boy thought *she* was a boy! George was always gracious to people who made the mistake of thinking she was a boy.

'Of *course* I'll take you!' she said. 'It shouldn't be long before I do – the experiment is nearly done.'

7

A little squabble

A sound made them turn. It was the boy's father coming up. He nodded to the children. 'Making friends?' he said, amiably. 'That's right. My boy's pretty lonely here. I hope you'll come up and see us some time. Finished your conversation, son?'

'Yes,' said the boy. 'This boy here says that island is his, and he's going to take me over it when his father has finished his work there – and that won't be long.'

'And do you know the way through all those wicked rocks?' said the man. '*I* shouldn't care to try it. I was talking to the fishermen the other day, and not one of them appeared to know the way!'

This was rather astonishing. Some of the fishermen *did* know it. Then the children remembered that the men had all been forbidden to take anyone to the island while Uncle Quentin was at work there. It was clear that they had pretended not to know the way, in loyalty to their orders.

'Did you want to go to the island then?' asked Dick, suddenly.

'Oh no! But my boy here would love to go,' said the man. '*I* don't want to be seasick, bobbing up and down on those waves near the island. I'm a poor sailor. I never go on the sea if I can help it!'

'Well, we must go,' said Julian. 'We've got to do some shopping for my aunt. Good-bye!'

'Come and see us as soon as you can,' said the man. 'I've a fine television set that Martin here would like to show you. Any afternoon you like!'

'Oh thanks!' said George. She seldom saw television. 'We'll come!'

They parted, and the four children and Timmy went on down the cliff-path.

'Whatever made you sound so rude, Dick?' said George. 'The way you said "What's that to do with you?" sounded quite insulting.'

'Well – I just felt suspicious, that's all,' said Dick. 'That boy seemed to be so jolly interested in the island and in your father's work, and when it would be finished.'

'Why shouldn't he be?' demanded George. 'Everyone in the village is interested. They all know about the tower. And all the boy wanted to know was when he could go to my island – that's why he asked when Father's work would be finished. I liked him.'

'You only liked him because he was ass enough to think you were a boy,' said Dick. 'Jolly girlish-looking boy you are, that's all I can say.'

George flared up at once. 'Don't be mean! I'm *not* girlish-looking. I've far more freckles than you have, for one thing, and better eyebrows. *And* I can make my voice go deep.'

'You're just silly,' said Dick, in disgust. 'As if freckles are boyish! Girls have them just as much as boys. I don't believe that boy thought you were a boy at all. He was just sucking up to you. He must have heard how much you like playing at being what you aren't.'

George walked up to Dick with such a furious look on her face that Julian hastily put himself in between them. 'Now, no brawls,' he said. 'You're both too old to begin slapping each other like kids in the nursery. Let me tell you, you're both behaving like babies, not like boys *or* girls!'

Anne was looking on with scared eyes. George didn't go off the deep end like this usually. And it *was* funny of Dick to have spoken so rudely to the boy on the cliff. Timmy gave a sudden little whine. His tail was down, and he looked very miserable.

'Oh George – Timmy can't *bear* you to quarrel with Dick!' said Anne. 'Look at him! He's just miserable!'

'He didn't like that boy a bit,' said Dick. 'That was another thing I thought was funny. If Timmy doesn't like a person, *I* don't like him either.'

'Timmy doesn't *always* rush round new people,' said George. 'He didn't growl or snarl, anyway. All right, all right, Julian; I'm not going to start brawling. But I do think Dick is being silly. Making a mountain out of a molehill – just because someone was interested in Kirrin Island and Father's work, and just because Timmy didn't caper all round him. He was such a solemn sort of boy that I'm not surprised Timmy wasn't all over him. He probably knew the boy wouldn't like it. Timmy's clever like that.'

'Oh, do stop,' said Dick. 'I give in – gracefully! I may be making a fuss. Probably am. I couldn't help my feelings, though.'

Anne gave a sigh of relief. The squabble was over. She hoped it wouldn't crop up again. George had been very touchy since she had been home. If only Uncle Quentin would hurry up and finish his work, and they could all go to the island as much as they liked, things would be all right.

'I'd rather like to see that television set,' said George.

'We might go up some afternoon.'

'Right,' said Julian. 'But on the whole, I think it would be best if we steered clear of any talk about your father's work. Not that we know much. Still, we do know that once before there were people after one of his theories. The secrets of the scentists are very, very important these days, you know, George. Scientists are VIP!'

'What's VIP?' asked Anne.

'Very Important People, baby!' said Julian, with a laugh. 'What did you think it meant? Violet, Indigo, Purple? I guess those are the colours Uncle Quentin would go if he knew anyone was trying to snoop into his secrets!'

Everyone laughed, even George. She looked affectionately at Julian. He was always so sensible and good-tempered. She really would go by what he said.

The day passed swiftly. The weather cleared and the sun came out strongly. The air smelt of gorse and prim-roses and the salt of the sea. Lovely! They went shopping for Aunt Fanny, and stopped to talk with James, the fisher-boy.

'Your father's got the island, I see,' he said to George with a grin. 'Bad luck, Miss. You'll not be going over there so often. And nobody else will, either, so I've heard.'

'That's right,' said George. 'Nobody is allowed to go over there for some time. Did you help to take some of the stuff over, James?'

'Yes. I know the way, you see, because I've been with you,' said James. 'Well, Miss, how did you find your boat when you went across yesterday? I got her all ship-shape for you, didn't I?'

'Yes, you did, James,' said George, warmly. 'You made her look beautiful. You must come across to the island with us next time we go.'

'Thanks,' said James, his ready grin showing all his

white teeth. 'Like to leave Timmy with me for a week or two? See how he wants to stay!'

George laughed. She knew James was only joking. He was very fond of Timmy, though, and Timmy adored James. He was now pushing himself hard against the fisher-boy's knees, and trying to put his nose into his brown hand. Timmy had never forgotten the time when James looked after him so well.

The evening came, and the bay was softly blue. Little white horses flecked it here and there. The four gazed across to Kirrin Island. It always looked so lovely at this time of the evening.

The glass top of the tower winked and blinked in the sun. It looked almost as if someone was signalling. But there was no one in the little glass room. As the children watched they heard a faint rumbling sound, and suddenly the top of the tower was ablaze with a curious glare.

'Look! That's what happened yesterday!' said Julian, in excitement. 'Your father's at work all right, George. I do wonder what he's doing!'

Then there came a throbbing sound, almost like the noise of an aeroplane, and once more the glass top of the tower shone and blazed, as the wires became full of some curious power.

'Weird,' said Dick. 'A bit frightening too. Where's your father at this very moment, I wonder, George. How I'd like to know!'

'I bet he's forgotten all about meals again,' said George. 'Didn't he wolf our sandwiches – he must have been starving. I wish he'd let Mother go over there and look after him.'

Her mother came in at that moment. 'Did you hear the noise?' she said. 'I suppose that was your father at work again. Oh dear, I hope he doesn't blow himself up one of these days!'

'Aunt Fanny, can I stay up till half past ten tonight?'

asked Anne, hopefully. 'To see Uncle Quentin's signal, you know?'

'Good gracious, no!' said her aunt. 'No one needs to stay up. I am quite capable of watching for it myself!'

'Oh Aunt Fanny! Surely I and Dick can stay up!' said Julian. 'After all, we're not in bed till ten at school.'

'Yes – but this is *half past* ten, and you wouldn't even be in bed then,' said his aunt. 'There's no reason why you shouldn't lie in bed and watch for it though, if you want to – providing you haven't fallen asleep!'

'Oh yes – I can do that,' said Julian. 'My window looks across to Kirrin Island. Six flashes with a lantern? I shall count them carefully.'

So the four went to bed at the usual time. Anne was asleep long before half past ten, and George was so drowsy that she could not make herself get up and go into the boys' room. But Dick and Julian were both wide awake. They lay in their beds and looked out of the window. There was no moon, but the sky was clear, and the stars shone down, giving a faint light. The sea looked very black. There was no sign of Kirrin Island. It was lost in the darkness of the night.

'Almost half past ten,' said Julian, looking at his watch which had luminous hands. 'Now then, Uncle Quentin, what about it?'

Almost as if his uncle was answering him, a light shone out in the glass top of the tower. It was a clear, small light, like the light of a lantern.

Julian began to count. 'One flash.' There was a pause. 'Two flashes.' Another pause 'Three . . . four . . . five . . .six!'

The flashes stopped. Julian snuggled down into bed. 'Well, that's that. Uncle Quentin's all right. I say, it's weird to think of him climbing that spiral stairway right to the top of the tower, in the dark of night, isn't it? – just to mess about with those wires.'

'Mmmmm,' said Dick sleepily. 'I'd rather he did it, than I! You can be a scientist if you like, Ju – but *I* don't want to climb towers in the dead of night on a lonely island. I'd like Timmy there, at least!'

Someone knocked on their door and it opened. Julian sat up at once. It was Aunt Fanny.

'Oh Julian dear – did you see the flashes? I forgot to count them. Were there six?'

'Oh yes, Aunt Fanny! I'd have rushed down to tell you if anything was wrong. Uncle's all right. Don't you worry!'

'I wish I'd told him to do an *extra* flash to tell me if he's had some of that nice soup,' said his aunt. 'Well, good night, Julian. Sleep well!'

8

Down in the quarry

The next day dawned bright and sunny. The four tore down to breakfast, full of high spirits. 'Can we bathe? Aunt Fanny, it's *really* warm enough! Oh do say we can!'

'Of course not! Whoever heard of bathing in April!' said Aunt Fanny. 'Why, the sea is terribly cold. Do you want to be in bed for the rest of the holiday with a chill?'

'Well, let's go for a walk on the moors at the back of Kirrin Cottage,' said George. 'Timmy would love that. Wouldn't you, Tim?'

'Woof,' said Timmy, thumping his tail hard on the ground.

'Take your lunch with you if you like,' said her mother. 'I'll pack some for you.'

'You'll be glad to be rid of us for a little while, I expect, Aunt Fanny,' said Dick, with a grin. 'I know what we'll do. We'll go to the old quarry and look for prehistoric weapons! We've got a jolly good museum at school, and I'd like to take back some stone arrowheads or something like that.'

They all liked hunting for things. It would be fun to go to the old quarry, and it would be lovely and warm in the hollow there.

'I hope we shan't find a poor dead sheep there, as we once did,' said Anne, with a shudder. 'Poor thing! It must have fallen down and baa-ed for help for ages.'

'Of course we shan't,' said Julian. 'We shall find stacks of primroses and violets though, growing down the sides of the quarry. They are always early there because it's sheltered from every wind.'

'I should love to have bunches of primroses,' said his aunt. 'Nice big ones! Enough to put all over the house.'

'Well, while the boys are looking for arrow-heads we'll look for primroses,' said Anne, pleased. 'I like picking flowers.'

'And Timmy, of course, will hunt for rabbits, and will hope to bring home enough for you to decorate the larder from top to bottom,' said Dick, solemnly. Timmy looked thrilled and gave an excited little woof.

They waited for Uncle Quentin's signal at half past ten. It came – six flashes of a mirror in the sun. The flashes were quite blinding.

'Nice little bit of heliographing!' said Dick. 'Good morning and good-bye, Uncle! We'll watch for you tonight. Now, everybody ready?'

'Yes! Come on, Tim! Who's got the sandwiches? I say, isn't the sun hot!'

Off they all went. It was going to be a really lovely day!

The quarry was not really very far – only about a quarter of a mile. The children went for a walk beforehand, for Timmy's sake. Then they made for the quarry.

It was a queer place. At some time or other it had been deeply quarried for stone, and then left to itself. Now the sides were covered with small bushes and grass and plants of all kinds. In the sandy places heather grew.

The sides were very steep, and as few people came there, there were no paths to follow. It was like a huge rough bowl, irregular in places, and full of colour now where primroses opened their pale petals to the sky. Violets grew there by the thousand, both white and purple. Cowslips were opening too, the earliest anywhere.

'Oh, it's lovely!' said Anne, stopping at the top and looking down. 'Simply super! I never in my life saw so many primroses – nor such huge ones!'

'Be careful how you go, Anne,' said Julian. 'These sides are very steep. If you lose your footing you'll roll right down to the bottom – and find yourself with a broken arm or leg!'

'I'll be careful,' said Anne. 'I'll throw my basket down to the bottom, so that I can have two hands to cling to bushes with, if I want to. I shall be able to fill that basket cramful of primroses and violets!'

She flung the basket down, and it bounced all the way to the bottom of the quarry. The children climbed down to where they wanted to go – the girls to a great patch of big primroses, the boys to a place where they thought they might find stone weapons.

'Hallo!' said a voice, suddenly, from much lower down. The four stopped in surprise, and Timmy growled.

'Why – it's you!' said George, recognizing the boy they had met the day before.

'Yes. I don't know if you know my name. It's Martin Curton,' said the boy.

Julian told him their names too. 'We've come to picnic here,' he said. 'And to see if we can find stone weapons. What have you come for?'

'Oh – to see if I can find stone weapons too,' said the boy.

'Have you found any?' asked George.

'No. Not yet.'

'Well, you won't find any just there,' said Dick. 'Not in heather! You want to come over here, where the ground is bare and gravelly.'

Dick was trying to be friendly, to make up for the day before. Martin came over and began to scrape about with the boys. They had trowels with them, but he had only his hands.

'Isn't it hot down here?' called Anne. 'I'm going to take off my coat.'

Timmy had his head and shoulders down a rabbit-hole. He was scraping violently, sending up heaps of soil behind him in a shower.

'Don't go near Timmy unless you want to be buried in earth!' said Dick. 'Hey, Timmy – is a rabbit really worth all that hard work?'

Apparently it was, for Timmy, panting loudly, went on digging for all he was worth. A stone flew high in the air and hit Julian. He rubbed his cheek. Then he looked at the stone that lay beside him. He gave a shout. 'Look at this – a jolly fine arrow-head! Thanks, Timmy, old fellow. Very good of you to go digging for me. What about a hammer-head next?'

The others came to see the stone arrow-head. Anne thought she would never have known what it was – but Julian and Dick exclaimed over it in admiration.

'Jolly good specimen,' said Dick. 'See how it's been shaped, George? To think that this was used thousands of years ago to kill the enemies of a cave-man!' Martin did not say much. He just looked at the arrow-head, which certainly was a very fine unspoilt specimen, and then turned away. Dick thought he was a queer fellow. A bit dull and boring. He wondered if they ought to ask him to their picnic. He didn't want to in the least.

But George did! 'Are you having a picnic here too?' she said. Martin shook his head.

'No. I've not brought any sandwiches.'

'Well, we've plenty. Stay and have some with us when we eat them,' said George, generously.

'Thanks. It's very nice of you,' said the boy. 'And will you come and see my television set this afternoon in return! I'd like you to.'

'Yes, we will,' said George. 'It would be something to do! Oh Anne – just look at those violets! I've never seen such big white ones before. Won't Mother be pleased?'

The boys went deeper down, scraping about with their trowels in any likely place. They came to where a shelf of stone projected out a good way. It would be a nice place to have their lunch. The stone would be warm to sit on, and was flat enough to take ginger-beer bottles and cups in safety.

At half past twelve they all had their lunch. They were very hungry. Martin shared their sandwiches, and became quite friendly over them.

'Best sandwiches I've ever tasted,' he said. 'I do like those sardine ones. Does your mother make them for you? I wish I had a mother. Mine died ages ago.'

There was a sympathetic silence. The four could not think of any worse thing to happen to a boy or girl. They offered Martin the nicest buns, and the biggest piece of cake immediately.

'I saw your father flashing his signals last night,' said Martin, munching a bun.

Dick looked up at once. 'How do you know he was signalling?' he asked. 'Who told you?'

'Nobody,' said the boy. 'I just saw the six flashes, and I thought it must be George's father.' He looked surprised at Dick's sharp tone. Julian gave Dick a nudge, to warn him not to go off the deep end again.

George scowled at Dick. 'I suppose you saw my father signalling this morning too,' she said to Martin. 'I bet scores of people saw the flashes. He just heliographs with a mirror at half past ten to signal that he's all right – and flashes a lantern at the same time at night.'

Now it was Dick's turn to scowl at George. Why give away all this information? It wasn't necessary. Dick felt sure she was doing it just to pay him out for his sharp question. He tried to change the subject.

'Where do you go to school?' he asked.

'I don't,' said the boy. 'I've been ill.'

'Well, where did you go to school before you were ill?' asked Dick.

I – I had a tutor,' said Martin. 'I didn't go to school.'

'Bad luck!' said Julian. He thought it must be terrible not to go to school and have all the fun, the work and the games of school-life. He looked curiously at Martin. Was he one of these rather stupid boys who did no good at school, but had to have a tutor at home? Still he didn't *look* stupid. He just looked rather sullen and dull.

Timmy was sitting on the warm stone with the others. He had his share of the sandwiches, but had to be rationed, as Martin had to have some too.

He was funny with Martin. He took absolutely no notice of him at all. Martin might not have been there!

And Martin took no notice of Timmy. He did not talk to him, or pat him. Anne was sure he didn't really like dogs, as he had said. How could anyone be with Timmy and not give him even *one* pat?

Timmy did not even look at Martin, but sat with his back to him, leaning against George. It was really rather amusing, if it wasn't so odd. After all, George was talking in a friendly way to Martin; they were all sharing their food with him – and Timmy behaved as if Martin simply wasn't there at all!

Anne was just about to remark on Timmy's odd behaviour when he yawned, shook himself, and leapt down from the rock. 'He's going rabbiting again,' said Julian.

'Hey, Tim – find me another arrow-head will you, old fellow?'

Timmy wagged his tail. He disappeared under the shelf of rock, and there came the sound of digging. A shower of stones and soil flew into the air.

The children lay back on the stone and felt sleepy. They talked for some minutes, and then Anne felt her eyes closing. She was awakened by George's voice.

'Where's Timmy? Timmy! Timmy! Come here! Where have you got to?'

But no Timmy came. There was not even an answering bark. 'Oh blow, said George. 'Now he's gone down some extra-deep rabbit hole, I suppose. I must get him. Timmy! Wherever are you?'

9

George makes a discovery – and loses her temper

George slipped down from the rock. She peered under it. There was a large opening there, scattered with stones that Timmy had loosened in his digging.

'Surely you haven't at last found a rabbit hole big enough to go down!' said George. 'TIMMY! Where are you?'

Not a bark, not a whine came from the hole. George wriggled under the shelf of rock, and peered down the burrow. Timmy had certainly made it very big. George called up to Julian.

'Julian! Throw me down your trowel, will you?'

The trowel landed by her foot. George took it and began to make the hole bigger. It might be big enough for Timmy, but it wasn't big enough for her!

She dug hard and soon got very hot. She crawled out and looked over on to the rock to see if she could get one of the others to help her. They were all asleep.

'Lazy things!' thought George, quite forgetting that she too would have been dozing if she hadn't wondered where Timmy had gone.

She slipped down under the rock again and began to dig hard with her trowel. Soon she had made the hole big enough to get through. She was surprised to find quite a large passage, once she had made the entrance big enough to take her. She could crawl along on hands and knees!

'I say – I wonder if this is just some animal's runway – or leads somewhere!' thought George. 'TIMMY! Where *are* you?'

From somewhere deep in the quarry side there came a faint whine. George felt thankful. So Timmy *was* there, after all. She crawled along, and then quite suddenly the tunnel became high and wide and she realized that she must be in a passage. It was perfectly dark, so she could not see anything, she could only feel.

Then she heard the sound of pattering feet, and Timmy pressed affectionately against her legs, whining. 'Oh Timmy – you gave me a bit of a fright!' said George. 'Where have you been? Is this a real passage – or just a tunnel in the quarry, made by the old miners, and now used by animals?'

'Woof,' said Timmy, and pulled at George's jeans to make her go back to the daylight.

'All right, I'm coming!' said George. 'Don't imagine I want to wander alone in the dark! I only came to look for you.'

She made her way back to the shelf of rock. By this time Dick was awake, and wondered where George had gone. He waited a few minutes, blinking up into the deep blue sky, and then sat up.

'George!' There was no answer. So, in his turn Dick slipped down from the rock and looked around. And, to his very great astonishment he saw first Timmy, and then George on hands and knees, appearing out of the hole under the rock. He stared open-mouthed, and George began to giggle.

'It's all right. I've only been rabbiting with Timmy!'

She stood beside him, shaking and brushing soil from her jersey and trousers. 'There's a passage behind the entrance to the hole under the rock,' she said. 'At first it's just a narrow tunnel, like an animal's hole – then it gets wider – and then it becomes a proper high wide passage! I couldn't see if it went on, of course, because it was dark. Timmy was a long way in.'

'Good gracious!' said Dick. 'It sounds exciting.'

'Let's explore it, shall we?' said George. 'I expect Julian's got a torch.'

'No,' said Dick. 'We won't explore today.'

The others were now awake, and listening with interest. 'Is it a secret passage?' said Anne, thrilled. 'Oh do let's explore it!'

'No, not today,' said Dick again. He looked at Julian. Julian guessed that Dick did not want Martin to share this secret. Why should he? He was not a real friend of theirs, and they had only just got to know him. He nodded back to Dick.

'No, we won't explore today. Anyway, it may be nothing – just an old tunnel made by the quarrymen.'

Martin was listening with great interest. He went and looked into the hole. 'I wish we could explore,' he said. 'Maybe we could plan to meet again with torches and see if there really is a passage there.'

Julian looked at his watch. 'Nearly two o'clock. Well, Martin, if we're going to see that half past two programme of yours, we'd better be getting on.'

Carrying baskets of primroses and violets, the girls

began to climb up the steep side of the quarry. Julian took Anne's basket from her, afraid she might slip and fall. Soon they were all at the top. The air felt quite cool there after the warmth of the quarry.

They made their way to the cliff path and before long were passing the coastguard's cottage. He was out in his garden, and he waved to them.

They went in the gateway of the next-door cottage. Martin pushed the door open. His father was sitting at the window of the room inside, reading. He got up with a broad, welcoming smile.

'Well, well, well! This *is* nice! Come along in, do. Yes, the dog as well. I don't mind dogs a bit. I like them.'

It seemed rather a crowd in the small room. They all shook hands politely. Martin explained hurriedly that he had brought the children to see a television programme.

'A good idea,' said Mr Curton, still beaming. Anne stared at his great eyebrows. They were very long and thick. She wondered why he didn't have them trimmed – but perhaps he liked them like that. They made him look very fierce, she thought.

The four looked round the little room. There was a television set standing at the far end, on a table. There was also a magnificent wireless – and something else that made the boys stare with interest.

'Hallo! You've got a transmitting set, as well as a receiving set,' said Julian.

'Yes,' said Mr Curton. 'It's a hobby of mine. I made that set.'

'Well! You must be brainy!' said Dick.

'What's a transmitting set?' asked Anne. 'I haven't heard of one before.'

'Oh, it just means a set to send out messages by wireless – like police-cars have, when they send back messages to the police stations,' said Dick. 'This is a very powerful one, though.'

Martin was fiddling about with the television switches. Then the programme began.

It was great fun seeing the television programme. When it was over Mr Curton asked them to stay to tea.

'Now don't say no,' he said. 'I'll ring up and ask your aunt, if you like, if you're afraid she might be worried.'

'Well – if you'd do that, sir,' said Julian. 'I think she *would* wonder where we'd gone!'

Mr Curton rang up Aunt Fanny. Yes, it was quite all right for them to stay, but they mustn't be too late back. So they settled down to an unexpectedly good tea. Martin was not very talkative, but Mr Curton made up for it. He laughed and joked and was altogether very good company.

The talk came round to Kirrin Island. Mr Curton said how beautiful it looked each evening. George looked pleased.

'Yes,' she said. '*I* always think that. I do wish Father hadn't chosen this particular time to work on my island. I'd planned to go and stay there.'

'I suppose you know every inch of it!' said Mr Curton.

'Oh yes!' said George. 'We all do. There are dungeons there, you know – real dungeons that go deep down – where we once found gold ingots.'

'Yes – I remember reading about that,' said Mr Curton. 'That must have been exciting. Fancy *finding* the dungeons too! And there's an old well too you once got down, isn't there?'

'Yes,' said Anne, remembering. 'And there is a cave where we once lived – it's got an entrance through the roof, as well as from the sea.'

'And I suppose your father is conducting his marvellous experiments down in the dungeons?' said Mr Curton. 'Well, what a strange place to work in!'

'No – we don't . . .' began George, when she got a kick on the ankle from Dick. She screwed up her face in pain. It had been a very sharp kick indeed.

'What were you going to say?' said Mr Curton, looking surprised.

'Er – I was just going to say that – er – er – we don't know which place Father has chosen,' said George, keeping her legs well out of the way of Dick's feet.

Timmy gave a sudden sharp whine. George looked down at him in surprise. He was looking up at Dick, with a very hurt expression.

'What's the matter, Timmy!' said George anxiously.

'He's finding the room too hot, I think,' said Dick. 'Better take him out, George.'

George, feeling quite anxious, took him out. Dick joined her. She scowled at him. 'What did you want to kick me for like that? I shall have a frightful bruise.'

'You know jolly well why I did,' said Dick. 'Giving away everything like that! Can't you see the chap's very interested in your father being on the island? There may be nothing in it at all, but you might at least keep your mouth shut. Just like a girl, can't help blabbing. I had to stop you somehow. I don't mind telling you I trod jolly hard on poor old Timmy's tail too, to make him yelp, so that you'd stop talking!'

'Oh – you beast!' said George, indignantly. 'How *could* you hurt Timmy?'

'I didn't want to. It was a shame,' said Dick, stopping to fondle Timmy's ears. 'Poor old Tim. I didn't want to hurt you, old fellow.'

'I'm going home,' said George, her face scarlet with anger. 'I hate you for talking to me like that – telling me I blab like a girl – and stamping on poor Timmy's tail. You can go back and say I'm taking Timmy home.'

'Right,' said Dick. 'And a jolly good thing too. The less you talk to Mr Curton the better. *I'm* going back to find out exactly what he is and what he does. I'm getting jolly suspicious. You'd better go before you give anything else away!'

Almost choking with rage, George went off with Timmy. Dick went back to make her apologies. Julian and Anne, sure that something was up, felt most uncomfortable. They rose to go, but to their surprise, Dick became very talkative and appeared to be suddenly very much interested in Mr Curton and what he did.

But at last they said good-bye and went. 'Come again, do,' said Mr Curton, beaming at the three of them. 'And tell the other boy – what's his name, George – that I hope his dog is quite all right again now. Such a nice, well-behaved dog! Well good-bye! See you again soon, I hope!'

10

A surprising signal

'What's up with George?' demanded Julian, as soon as they were safely out of earshot. 'I know you kicked her at tea-time, for talking too much about the island – that was idiotic of her – but why has she gone home in a huff?'

Dick told them how he had trodden on poor Timmy's tail to make him whine, so that George would turn her attention to him and stop talking. Julian laughed, but Anne was indignant.

'That was *horrid* of you, Dick.'

'Yes, it was,' said Dick. 'But I couldn't think of any other way to head George off the island. I really honestly thought she was giving away to that fellow all the things he badly wanted to know. But now I think he wanted to know them for quite another reason.'

'What do you mean?' said Julian puzzled.

'Well, I thought at first he must be after Uncle Quentin's secret, whatever it is,' said Dick, 'and that was why he wanted to know all the ins and outs of everything. But now that he's told me he's a journalist – that's a man who writes for the newspapers, Anne – I think after all he only wants the information so that he can use it for his paper, and make a splash when Uncle has finished his work.'

'Yes, I think that too,' said Julian thoughtfully; 'in fact, I'm pretty sure of it. Well, there's no harm in that but I don't see why we should sit there and be pumped all the time. He could easily say, "Look here, I'd be obliged if you'd spill the beans about Kirrin Island – I want to use it in a newspaper story." But he didn't say that.'

'No. So I was suspicious,' said Dick. 'But I see now he'd want all sorts of tit-bits about Kirrin Island to put in his newspaper, whatever it is. Blow! Now I shall have to explain to George I was wrong – and she really is in a temper!'

'Let's take the road to Kirrin Village and go to get some bones for Timmy at the butcher's,' said Julian. 'A sort of apology to Tim!'

This seemed a good idea. They bought two large meaty bones at the butcher's, and then went to Kirrin Cottage. George was up in her bedroom with Timmy. The three went up to find her.

She was sitting on the floor with a book. She looked up sulkily as they came in.

'George, sorry I was such a beast,' said Dick. 'I did it in a good cause, if you only knew it. But I've discovered that Mr Curton isn't a spy, seeking out your father's secret – he's only a journalist, smelling out a story for his paper! Look – I've brought these for Timmy – I apologize to him too.'

George was in a very bad temper, but she tried to respond to Dick's friendliness. She gave him a small smile.

'All right. Thanks for the bones. Don't talk to me tonight anybody. I feel mad, but I'll get over it.'

They left her sitting on the floor. It was always best to leave George severely alone when she was in one of her tempers. As long as Timmy was with her, she was all right, and he certainly would not leave her while she was cross and unhappy.

George did not come down to supper. Dick explained. 'We had a bit of a row, Aunt Fanny, but we've made it up. George still feels sore about it though. Shall I take her supper up?'

'No, I will,' said Anne, and she took up a tray of food.

'I'm not hungry,' said George, so Anne prepared to take it away again. 'Well, you can leave it,' said George hurriedly. 'I expect Timmy will like it.'

So Anne, with a secret smile to herself left the tray. All the dishes were empty by the time she climbed the stairs to fetch the tray again!

'Dear me – Timmy *was* hungry!' she said to George, and her cousin smiled sheepishly. 'Aren't you coming down now? We're going to play monopoly.'

'No thanks. You leave me alone this evening, and I'll be all right tomorrow,' said George. 'Really I will.'

So Julian, Dick, Anne and Aunt Fanny played monopoly without George. They went up to bed at the usual time and found George in bed, fast asleep, with Timmy curled up on her toes.

'I'll look out for Uncle Quentin's signal,' said Julian, as he got into bed. 'Gosh, it's a dark night tonight.'

He lay in bed and looked out of the window towards Kirrin Island. Then, at exactly half past ten, the six flashes came – flash, flash, flash, through the darkness. Julian buried his head in his pillow. Now for a good sleep!

He was awakened by a throbbing noise some time later. He sat up and looked out of the window, expecting to see the top of the tower ablaze with light, as it sometimes was when his uncle conducted a special experiment. But nothing happened. There was no flare of light. The throbbing died away and Julian lay down again.

'I saw Uncle's signals all right last night, Aunt Fanny,' he said next morning. 'Did you?'

'Yes,' said his aunt. 'Julian, do you think you would watch for them this morning, dear? I have to go and see the vicar about something, and I don't believe I should be able to see the tower from the vicarage.'

'Yes, of course I will, Aunt Fanny,' said Julian. 'What's the time now? Half past nine. Right. I'll write some letters sitting by the window in my room – and at half past ten I'll watch for the signals.'

He wrote his letters interrupted first by Dick, then by George, Anne and Timmy, who wanted him to go on the beach with them. George had quite recovered herself now, and was trying to be specially nice to make up for yesterday's temper.

'I'll come at half past ten,' said Julian. 'After I've seen the signals from the tower. They're due in ten minutes.'

At half past ten he looked at the glass top of the tower. Ah – there was the first signal, blazing brightly as the sun caught the mirror held by his uncle in the tower.

'One flash,' counted Julian. 'Two – three – four – five – six. He's all right.'

He was just about to turn away when another flash caught his eyes. 'Seven!' Then another came. Eight. Nine. Ten. Eleven. Twelve.

'How queer,' said Julian. 'Why twelve flashes? Hallo here we go again!'

Another six flashes came from the tower, then no more at all. Julian wished he had a telescope, then he could see right into the tower! He sat and thought for a moment, puzzled. Then he heard the others come pounding up the stairs. They burst into the room.

'Julian! Father flashed eighteen times instead of six!'

'Did you count them, Ju?'

'Why did he do that? Is he in danger of some sort?'

'No. If he was he'd flash the SOS signal,' said Julian.

'He doesn't know Morse!' said George.

'Well, I expect he just wants to let us know that he needs something,' said Julian. 'We must go over today and find out what it is. More food perhaps.'

So, when Aunt Fanny came home they suggested they should all go over to the island. Aunt Fanny was pleased.

'Oh yes! That would be nice. I expect your uncle wants a message sent off somewhere. We'll go this morning.'

George flew off to tell James she wanted her boat. Aunt Fanny packed up plenty of food with Joanna's help. Then they set off to Kirrin Island in George's boat.

As they rounded the low wall of rocks and came into the little cove, they saw Uncle Quentin waiting for them. He waved his hand, and helped to pull in the boat when it ran gently on to the sand.

'We saw your treble signal,' said Aunt Fanny. 'Did you want something, dear?'

'Yes, I did,' said Uncle Quentin. 'What's that you've got in your basket, Fanny? More of those delicious sandwiches. I'll have some!'

'Oh Quentin – haven't you been having your meals properly again?' said Aunt Fanny. 'What about that lovely soup?'

'What soup?' said Uncle Quentin, looking surprised. 'I wish I'd known about it. I could have done with some last night.'

'But *Quentin*! I told you about it before,' said Aunt Fanny. 'It will be bad by now. You must pour it away. Now don't forget – pour it away! Where is it? Perhaps I had better pour it away myself.'

'No. I'll do it,' said Uncle Quentin. 'Let's sit down and have our lunch.'

It was much too early for lunch, but Aunt Fanny at once sat down and began to unpack the food. The children were always ready for a meal at any time, so they didn't in the least mind lunch being so early.

'Well, dear – how is your work getting on?' asked Aunt

Fanny, watching her husband devour sandwich after sandwich. She began to wonder if he had had anything at all to eat since she had left him two days ago.

'Oh very well indeed,' said her husband. 'Couldn't be better. Just got to a most tricky and interesting point. I'll have another sandwich, please.'

'Why did you signal eighteen times, Uncle Quentin?' asked Anne.

'Ah, well – it's difficult to explain, really,' said her uncle. 'The fact is – I can't help feeling there's somebody else on this island besides myself!'

'*Quentin!* What in the world do you mean?' cried Aunt Fanny, in alarm. She looked over her shoulder as if she half expected to see somebody there. All the children stared in amazement at Uncle Quentin.

He took another sandwich. 'Yes, I know it sounds mad. Nobody else could possibly have got here. But I know there *is* someone!'

'Oh don't Uncle!' said Anne, with a shiver. 'It sounds horrid. And you're all alone at night too!'

'Ah, that's just it! I wouldn't mind a bit if I *was* all alone at night!' said her uncle. 'What worries me is that I don't think I *shall* be all alone.'

'Uncle, what makes you think there's somebody here?' asked Julian.

'Well, when I had finished the experiment I was doing last night – about half past three in the early morning it would be – but pitch dark, of course,' said Uncle Quentin, 'I came into the open for a breath of fresh air. And I could swear I heard somebody cough – yes, cough twice!'

'Good gracious!' said Aunt Fanny, startled. 'But Quentin – you might have been mistaken. You do imagine things sometimes, you know, when you're tired.'

'Yes, I know,' said her husband. 'But I couldn't imagine *this,* could I?'

He put his hand into his pocket and took something out.

He showed it to the others. It was a cigarette end, quite crisp and fresh.

'Now, I don't smoke cigarettes. Nor do any of you! Well then – who smoked that cigarette? And how did he come here? No one would bring him by boat – and that's the only way here.'

There was a silence. Anne felt scared. George stared at her father, puzzled. Who could be here? And why? And how had they got there?

'Well, Quentin – what are you going to do?' said his wife. 'What would be best?'

'I'll be all right if George will give her consent to something,' said Uncle Quentin. 'I want Timmy here, George! Will you leave him behind with me?'

11

George makes a hard choice

There was a horrified silence. George stared at her father in complete dismay. Everyone waited to see what she would say.

'But Father – Timmy and I have never been separated once,' she said at last, in a pleading voice. 'I do see you want him to guard you – and you *can* have him – but I'll have to stay here too!'

'Oh no!' said her father at once. 'You can't possibly stay, George. That's out of the question. As for never being separated from Timmy, well surely you wouldn't mind that for once? If it was to ensure my safety?'

George swallowed hard. This was the most difficult decision she had ever had to make in her life. Leave Timmy behind on the island – where there was some unknown hidden enemy, likely to harm him if he possibly could!

And yet there was Father too – he might be in danger if there was no one to guard him.

'I shall just *have* to stay here, Father,' she said. 'I can't leave Timmy behind unless I stay too. It's no good.'

Her father began to lose his temper. He was like George – he wanted his own way, and if he didn't have it he was going to make a fuss!

'If I'd asked Julian or Dick or Anne this same thing, and they'd had a dog, they would all have said yes, at once!' he raged. 'But you, George, you must always make things difficult if you can! You and that dog – anyone would think he was worth a thousand pounds!'

'He's worth much more than that to me,' said George, in a trembling voice. Timmy crept nearer to her and pushed his nose into her hand. She held his collar as if she would not let him go for a moment.

'Yes. That dog's worth more to you than your father or mother or anyone,' said her father, in disgust.

'No, Quentin, I can't have you saying things like that,' said his wife, firmly. 'That's just silly. A mother and father are quite different from a dog – they're loved in different ways. But you are perfectly right, of course – Timmy *must* stay behind with you – and I shall certainly not allow George to stay with him. I'm not going to have *both* of you exposed to danger. It's bad enough to worry about *you*, as it is.'

George looked at her mother in dismay.

'Mother! Do tell father I must stay here with Timmy.'

'Certainly not,' said her mother. 'Now George, be unselfish. If it were left to Tim to decide, you know perfectly well that he would stay here – and stay *without* you. He would say to himself, "I'm needed here – my eyes are needed to spy out enemies, my ears to hear a quiet footfall – and maybe my teeth to protect my master. I shall be parted from George for a few days – but she, like me, is big enough to put up with that!" That's what Timmy would say, George, if it were left to him.'

Everyone had been listening to this unexpected speech with great attention. It was about the only one that could persuade George to give in willingly!

She looked at Timmy. He looked back at her, wagging his tail. Then he did an extraordinary thing – he got up, walked over to George's father, and lay down beside him, looking at George as if to say 'There you are! Now you know what *I* think is right!'

'You see?' said her mother. 'He agrees with me. You've always said that Timmy was a good dog, and this proves it. He knows what his duty is. You ought to be proud of him.'

'I am,' said George, in a choky voice. She got up and walked off. 'All right,' she said over her shoulder. 'I'll leave him on the island with Father. I'll come back in a minute.'

Anne got up to go after poor George, but Julian pulled her down again. 'Leave her alone! She'll be all right. Good old Timmy – you know what's right and what's wrong, don't you? Good dog, splendid dog!'

Timmy wagged his tail. He did not attempt to follow George. No – he meant to stay by her father now, even though he would much rather be with his mistress. He was sorry that George was unhappy – but sometimes it was better to do a hard thing and be unhappy about it, than try to be happy without doing it.

'Oh Quentin dear, I don't like this business of you being here and somebody else spying on you,' said his wife, 'I really don't. How long will you be before you've finished your work?'

'A few days more,' said her husband. He looked at Timmy admiringly. 'That dog might almost have known what you were saying, Fanny, just now. It was remarkable the way he walked straight over to me.'

75

'He's a very clever dog,' said Anne warmly. 'Aren't you, Tim? You'll be quite safe with him, Uncle Quentin. He's terribly fierce when he wants to be!'

'Yes. I shouldn't care to have him leaping at *my* throat,' said her uncle. 'He's so big and powerful. Are there any more pieces of cake?'

'Quentin, it's really too bad of you to go without your meals,' said his wife. 'It's no good telling me you haven't, because you wouldn't be as ravenous as this if you had had your food regularly.'

Her husband took no notice of what she was saying. He was looking up at his tower. 'Do you ever see those wires at the top blaze out?' he asked. 'Wonderful sight, isn't it?'

'Uncle, you're not inventing a new atom bomb, or anything are you?' asked Anne.

Her uncle looked at her scornfully. 'I wouldn't waste my time inventing things that will be used to kill and maim people! No – I'm inventing something that will be of the greatest use to mankind. You wait and see!'

George came back. 'Father,' she said, 'I'm leaving Timmy behind for you – but please will you do something for me?'

'What?' asked her father. 'No silly conditions now! I shall feed Timmy regularly, and look after him, if that's what you want to ask me. I may forget my own meals, but you ought to know me well enough to know I shouldn't neglect any animal dependent on me.'

'Yes – I know, Father,' said George, looking a bit doubtful all the same. 'What I wanted to ask you was this – when you go up in the tower to signal each morning, will you please take Timmy with you? I shall be up at the coastguard's cottage, looking through his telescope at the glass room in the tower – and I shall be able to see Timmy then. If I catch just a glimpse of him each day and know he's all right, I shan't worry so much.'

'Very well,' said her father. 'But I don't suppose for a

moment that Timmy will be able to climb up the spiral stairway.'

'Oh, he can, Father – he's been up it once already,' said George.

'Good heavens!' said her father. 'Has the dog been up there too? All right, George – I promise I'll take him up with me each morning that I signal, and get him to wag his tail at you. There! Will that satisfy you?'

'Yes. Thank you,' said George. 'And you'll give him a few kind words and a pat occasionally, Father, won't you . . . and . . .?'

'And put his bib on for him at meal-times, I suppose, and clean his teeth for him at night!' said her father, looking cross again. 'I shall treat Timmy like a proper

grown-up dog, a friend of mine, George – and believe me, that's the way he wants me to treat him. Isn't it, Timmy? You like all those frills to be kept for your mistress, don't you, not for me?'

'Woof,' said Timmy, and thumped his tail. The children looked at him admiringly. He really was a very sensible clever dog. He seemed somehow much more grown-up than George.

'Uncle, if anything goes wrong, or you want help or anything, flash eighteen times again,' said Julian. 'You ought to be all right with Timmy. He's better than a dozen policemen – but you never know.'

'Right. Eighteen flashes if I want you over here for anything,' said his uncle. 'I'll remember. Now you'd better all go. It's time I got on with my work.'

'You'll pour that soup away, won't you, Quentin?' said his wife, anxiously. 'You don't want to make yourself ill by eating bad soup. It must be green by now! It would be so like you to forget all about it while it was fresh and good – and only remember when it was bad!'

'What a thing to say!' said her husband, getting up. 'Anyone would think I was five years old, without a brain in my head, the way you talk to me!'

'You've plenty of brains dear, we all know that,' said his wife. 'But you don't seem very old sometimes! Now look after yourself – and keep Timmy by you all the time.'

'Father won't need to bother about *that*,' said George. 'Timmy will keep by *him*! You're on guard, Timmy, aren't you? And you know what *that* means!'

'Woof,' said Timmy, solemnly. He went with them all to the boat, but he did not attempt to get in. He stood by George's father and watched the boat bob away over the water. 'Good-bye, Timmy!' shouted George, in a funny fierce voice. 'Look after yourself!'

Her father waved, and Timmy wagged his tail. George

took one of the pairs of oars from Dick and began to row furiously, her face red with the hard work.

Julian looked at her in amusement. It was hard work for him, too, to keep up with the furious rowing, but he didn't say anything. He knew all this fury in rowing was George's way of hiding her grief at parting with Timmy. Funny old George! She was always so intense about things – furiously happy or furiously unhappy, in the seventh heaven of delight or down in the very depths of despair or anger.

Everyone talked hard so that George would think they were not noticing her feelings at parting with Timmy. The talk, of course, was mostly about the unknown man on the island. It seemed very mysterious indeed that he should suddenly have arrived.

'How did he get there? I'm sure not one of the fishermen would have taken him,' said Dick. 'He must have gone at night, of course, and I doubt if there is anyone but George who would know the way in the dark – or even dare to try and find it. These rocks are so close together, and so near the surface; one yard out of the right course and any boat would have a hole in the bottom!'

'No one could reach the island by swimming from the shore,' said Anne. 'It's too far, and the sea is too rough over these rocks. I honestly do wonder if there *is* anyone on the island after all. Perhaps that cigarette end was an old one.'

'It didn't look it,' said Julian. 'Well, it just beats me how anyone got there!'

He fell into thought, puzzling out all the possible and impossible ways. Then he gave an exclamation. The others looked at him.

'I've just thought – would it be possible for an aeroplane to parachute anyone down on the island? I did hear a throbbing noise one night – was it last night? It must have been a plane's engine, of course! *Could* anyone be dropped on the island?'

'Easily,' said Dick. 'I believe you've hit on the explanation, Ju! Good for you! But I say – whoever it is must be in deadly earnest, to risk being dropped on a small island like that in the dark of night!'

In deadly earnest! That didn't sound at all nice. A little shiver went down Anne's back. 'I *am* glad Timmy's there,' she said. And everyone felt the same – yes even George!

12

The old map again

It was only about half past one when they arrived back, because they had had lunch so very early, and had not stayed long on the island. Joanna was most surprised to see them.

'Well, here you are again!' she said. 'I hope you don't all want another lunch, because there's nothing in the house till I go to the butcher's!'

'Oh no, Joanna – we've had our picnic lunch,' said her mistress, 'and it was a good thing we packed so much, because the master ate quite half of the lunch! He still hasn't had that nice soup we made for him. Now it will be bad of course.'

'Oh, the men! They're as bad as children!' said Joanna.

'*Well!*' said George. 'Do you really think any of *us* would let your good soup go bad, Joanna? You know jolly well we'd probably eat it up before we ought to!'

'That's true – I wouldn't accuse any of you four – or Timmy either – of playing about with your food,' said

Joanna. 'You make good work of it, the lot of you. But where is Timmy?'

'I left him behind to look after Father,' said George. Joanna stared at her in surprise. She knew how passionately fond of Timmy George was.

'You're a very good girl – sometimes!' she said. 'See now – if you're still hungry because your father has eaten most of your lunch, you go and look in the biscuit tin. I made you some of your favourite ginger biscuits this morning. You go and find them.'

That was always Joanna's way! If she thought anyone was upset, she offered them her best and freshest food. George went off to find the biscuits.

'You're a kind soul, Joanna,' said George's mother. 'I'm so thankful we left Timmy there. I feel happier about the master now.'

'What shall we do this afternoon?' said Dick, when they had finished munching the delicious ginger biscuits. 'I say, aren't these good? You know, I do think good cooks deserve some kind of decoration, just as much as good soldiers or scientists, or writers. I should give Joanna the OBCBE.'

'Whatever's that?' said Julian.

'Order of the Best Cooks of the British Empire,' said Dick grinning. 'What did you think it was? "Oh Be Careful Before Eating"?'

'You really are an absolute donkey,' said Julian. 'Now, what *shall* we do this afternoon?'

'Go and explore the passage in the quarry,' said George.

Julian cocked an eye at the window. 'It's about to pour with rain,' he said. 'I don't think that clambering up and down the steep sides of that quarry in the wet would be very easy. No – we'll leave that till a fine day.'

'I'll tell you what we'll do,' said Anne suddenly. 'Do you remember that old map of Kirrin Castle we once found in

82

a box? It had plans of the castle in it – a plan of the dungeons, and of the ground floor, and of the top part. Well, let's have it out and study it! Now we know there is another hiding-place somewhere, we might be able to trace it on that old map. It's sure to be on it somewhere – but perhaps we didn't notice it before!'

The others looked at her, thrilled. 'Now that really is a brilliant idea of yours, Anne,' said Julian, and Anne glowed with pleasure at his praise. 'A very fine idea indeed. Just the thing for a wet afternoon. Where's the map? I suppose you've got it somewhere safe, George?'

'Oh yes,' said George. 'It's still in that old wooden box, inside the tin lining. I'll get it.'

She disappeared upstairs and came down again with the map. It was made of thick parchment, and was yellow with age. She laid it out on the table. The others bent over it, eager to look at it once more.

'Do you remember how frightfully excited we were when we first found the box?' said Dick.

'Yes, and we couldn't open it, so we threw it out of the top window down to the ground below, hoping it would burst open!' said George.

'And the crash woke up Uncle Quentin,' said Anne, with a giggle. 'And he came out and got the box and wouldn't let us have it!'

'Oh dear yes – and poor Julian had to wait till Uncle Quentin was asleep, and creep in and get the box to see what was in it!' finished Dick. 'And we found this map – and how we pored over it!'

They all pored over it again. It was in three parts, as Anne had said – a plan of the dungeons, a plan of the ground floor and a plan of the top part.

'It's no good bothering about the top part of the castle,' said Dick. 'It's all fallen down and ruined. There's practically none of it left except for that one tower.'

'I say!' said Julian, suddenly putting his finger on a

certain spot in the map, 'do you remember there were *two* entrances to the dungeons? One that seemed to start somewhere about that little stone room – and the other that started where we did at last find the entrance? Well – we never found the other entrance, did we?'

'No! We didn't!' said George, in excitement. She pushed Julian's finger away from the map. 'Look – there are steps shown here – somewhere where that little room is – so there *must* be an entrance there! Here's the *other* flight of steps – the ones we did find, near the well.'

'I remember that we hunted pretty hard for the entrance in the little room,' said Dick. 'We scraped away the weeds from every single stone, and gave it up at last. Then we found the other entrance, and forgot all about this one.'

'And *I* think Father has found the entrance we *didn't* find!' said George, triumphantly. 'It leads underground, obviously. Whether or not it joins up with the dungeons we know I can't make out from this map. It's a bit blurred here. But it's quite plain that there *is* an entrance here, with stone steps leading underground somewhere! See, there's some sort of passage or tunnel marked, leading from the steps. Goodness knows where it goes, it's so smeared.'

'It joins up with the dungeons, I expect,' said Julian. 'We never explored the whole of them, you know – they're so vast and weird. If we explored the whole place, we should probably come across the stone steps leading from somewhere near that little room. Still, they may be ruined or fallen in now.'

'No, they can't be,' said George. 'I'm perfectly *sure* that's the entrance Father has found. And I'll tell you something that seems to prove it, too.'

'What?' said everyone.

'Well, do you remember the other day when we first went to see Father?' said George. 'He didn't let us stay long, and he came to see us off at the boat. Well, we tried to

84

see where he went, but we couldn't – but Dick said he saw the jackdaws rising up in a flock, as if they had been suddenly disturbed – and he wondered if Father had gone somewhere in that direction.'

Julian whistled. 'Yes – the jackdaws build in the tower, which is by the little room – and anyone going into the room would disturb them. I believe you're right, George.'

'It's been puzzling me awfully where Uncle Quentin could be doing his work,' said Dick. 'I simply could *not* solve the mystery – but now I think we have!'

'I wonder how Father found his hiding-place,' said George, thoughtfully. 'I still think it was mean of him not to tell me.'

'There must have been some reason,' said Dick, sensibly. 'Don't start brooding again!'

'I'm not,' said George. 'I'm puzzled, that's all. I wish we could take the boat and go over to the island at once, and explore!'

'Yes. I bet we'd find the entrance all right now,' said Dick. 'Your father is sure to have left some trace of where it is – a stone a bit cleaner than the rest – or weeds scraped off – or something.'

'Do you suppose the unknown enemy on the island knows Uncle Quentin's hiding-place?' said Anne, suddenly. 'Oh, I do hope he doesn't! He could so easily shut him in if he did.'

'Well, he hasn't gone there to shut Uncle up – he's gone there to steal his secret, or find it out,' said Julian. 'Golly, I'm thankful he's got Timmy. Timmy could tackle a dozen enemies.'

'Not if they had guns,' said George, in a small voice. There was a silence. It was not a nice thought to think of Timmy at the wrong end of a gun. This had happened once or twice before in their adventures, and they didn't want to think of it happening again.

'Well, it's no good thinking silly things like that,' said Dick, getting up. 'We've had a jolly interesting half-hour. I think we've solved *that* mystery. But I suppose we shan't know for certain till your father's finished his experiment, George, and left the island – then we can go over and have a good snoop round.'

'It's still raining,' said Anne, looking out of the window. 'But it's a bit clearer. It looks as if the sun will be out soon. Let's go for a walk.'

'I shall go up to the coastguard's cottage,' said George, at once. 'I want to look through his telescope to see if I can just get a glimpse of Timmy.'

'Try the field-glasses,' suggested Julian. 'Go up to the top of the house with them.'

'Yes, I will,' said George. 'Thanks for the idea.'

She fetched the field-glasses, where they hung in the hall, and took them out of their leather case. She ran upstairs with them. But she soon came down again, looking disappointed.

'The house isn't high enough for me to see much of the island properly. I can see the glass top of the tower easily, of course – but the telescope would show it much better. It's more powerful. I think I'll go up and have a squint. You don't need to come if you don't want to.' She put the glasses back into their case.

'Oh, we'll all come and have a squint for old Timmy dog,' said Dick, getting up. 'And I don't mind telling you what we'll see!'

'What?' said George, in surprise.

'We'll see Timmy having a perfectly wonderful time, chasing every single rabbit on the island!' said Dick with a grin. 'My word – you needn't worry about Timmy not having his food regularly! He'll have rabbit for breakfast, rabbit for dinner, rabbit for tea – and rain-water from his favourite pool. Not a bad life for old Timmy!'

'You know perfectly well he'll do nothing of the sort,'

said George. 'He'll keep close to Father and not think of rabbits once!'

'You don't know Timmy if you think that,' said Dick dodging out of George's way. She was turning red with exasperation. 'I bet that's why he wanted to stay. *Just* for the rabbits!'

George threw a book at him. It crashed to the floor. Anne giggled. 'Oh stop it, you two. We'll never get out. Come on Ju – we won't wait for the squabblers!'

13

Afternoon with Martin

By the time they reached the coastguard's cottage the sun was out. It was a real April day, with sudden showers and then the sun sweeping out, smiling. Everything glittered, especially the sea. It was wet underfoot, but the children had on their rubber boots.

They looked for the coastguard. As usual he was in his shed, singing and hammering.

'Good-day to you,' he said, beaming all over his red face. 'I was wondering when you'd come and see me again. How do you like this railway station I'm making?'

'It's better than any I've ever seen in the shops,' said Anne in great admiration. The coastguard certainly had made it well, down to the smallest detail.

He nodded his head towards some small wooden figures of porters and guards and passengers. 'Those are waiting to be painted,' he said. 'That boy Martin said he'd come in and do them for me – very handy with his paints he is, a proper artist – but he's had an accident.'

'*Has* he? What happened?' said Julian.

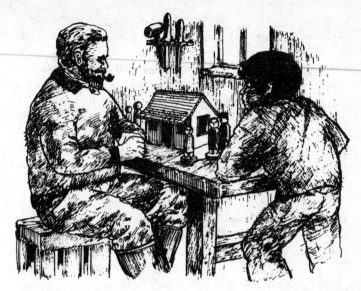

'I don't quite know. He was half-carried home this morning by his father,' said the coastguard. 'Must have slipped and fallen somewhere. I went out to ask, but Mr Curton was in a hurry to get the boy on a couch. Why don't you go in and ask after him? He's a queer sort of boy – but he's not a bad boy.'

'Yes, we will go and ask,' said Julian. 'I say, coast-guard – would you mind if we looked through your tele-scope again?'

'Now you go and look at all you want to!' said the old fellow. 'I tell you, you won't wear it out by looking! I saw the signal from your father's tower last night, Miss George – just happened to be looking that way. He went on flashing for a long time, didn't he?'

'Yes,' said George. 'Thank you. I'll go and have a look now.'

She went to the telescope and trained it on her island. But no matter where she looked she could not see Timmy, or her father. They must be down in his workroom, wherever it was. She looked at the glass room in the top of the tower. That was empty too, of course. She sighed. It would have been nice to see Timmy.

The others had a look through as well. But nobody saw Timmy. It was plain that he was keeping close to his master – a proper little guard!

'Well – shall we go in and see what's happened to Martin?' said Julian, when they had finished with the telescope. 'It's just about to pour with rain again – another April shower! We could wait next door till it's over.'

'Right, Let's go,' said Dick. He looked at George. 'Don't be afraid I shall be rude, George. Now that I know Mr Curton is a journalist, I shan't bother about him.'

'All the same – I'm not "blabbing" any more,' said George, with a grin. 'I see your point now – even if it doesn't matter, I still shan't "blab" any more.'

'Good for you!' said Dick, pleased. 'Spoken like a boy!'

'Ass!' said George, but she was pleased all the same.

They went through the front gateway of the next cottage. As they filed in, they heard an angry voice.

'Well, you can't! Always wanting to mess about with a brush and paint. I thought I'd knocked that idea out of your head. You lie still and get that ankle better. Spraining it just when I want your help!'

Anne stopped, feeling frightened. It was Mr Curton's voice they could hear through the open window. He was giving Martin a good talking to about something, that was plain. The others stopped too, wondering whether to go in or not.

Then they heard a bang, and saw Mr Curton leaving the cottage from the back entrance. He walked rapidly down the garden, and made for the path, that led to the back of the cliff. There was a road there that went to the village.

'Good. He's gone. *And* he didn't see us!' said Dick. 'Who

would have thought that such a genial, smiling fellow could have such a rough brutal voice when he loses his temper? Come on – let's pop in and see poor Martin while there's a chance.'

They knocked on the door. 'It's us!' called Julian, cheerfully. 'Can we come in?'

'Oh yes!' shouted Martin from indoors, sounding pleased. Julian opened the door and they all went in.

'I say! We heard you'd had an accident,' said Julian. 'What's up? Are you hurt much?'

'No. It's just that I twisted my ankle, and it was so painful to walk on that I had to be half-carried up here,' said Martin. 'Silly thing to do!'

'Oh – it'll soon be right if it's just a twist,' said Dick. 'I've often done that. The thing is to walk on it as soon as you can. Where were you when you fell?'

Martin went suddenly red, to everyone's surprise. 'Well – I was walking on the edge of the quarry with my father – and I slipped and rolled a good way down,' he said.

There was a silence. Then George spoke. 'I say,' she said, 'I hope you didn't go and give away our little secret to your father? I mean – it's not so much fun when grown-ups share a secret. They want to go snooping about themselves – and it's much more fun to discover things by ourselves. You didn't tell him about that hole under the shelf of rock, did you?'

Martin hesitated. 'I'm afraid I did,' he said at last. 'I didn't think it would matter. I'm sorry.'

'Blow!' said Dick. 'That was our own little discovery. We wanted to go and explore it this afternoon, but we thought it would be so wet we'd fall down the steep slope.'

Julian looked at Martin sharply. 'I suppose that's what happened to *you*?' he said. 'You tried clambering down and slipped!'

'Yes,' said Martin. 'I'm really sorry if you thought it

91

was your secret. I just mentioned it to my father out of interest – you know – something to say – and he wanted to go down and see for himself.'

'I suppose journalists are always like that,' said Dick. 'Wanting to be on the spot if there's anything to be ferreted out. It's their job. All right, Martin – forget it. But do try and head your father off the quarry. We *would* like to do a bit of exploring, before he butts in. Though there may be nothing to be found at all!'

There was a pause. Nobody knew quite what to say. Martin was rather difficult to talk to. He didn't talk like any ordinary boy – he never made a joke, or said anything silly.

'Aren't you bored, lying here?' said Anne feeling sorry for him.

'Yes, awfully. I wanted my father to go in and ask the coastguard to bring in some little figures I said I'd paint for him,' said Martin. 'But he wouldn't let me. You know I simply love painting – even doing a little thing like that – painting clothes on toy porters and guards – so long as I can have a brush in my hand and colours to choose from!'

This was the longest speech Martin had ever made to the four children! His face lost its dull, bored look as he spoke, and became bright and cheerful.

'O – you want to be an artist, I suppose?' said Anne. 'I would like that too!'

'Anne! you can't even draw a cat that looks like one!' said Dick, scornfully. 'And when you drew a cow I thought it was an elephant.'

Martin smiled at Anne's indignant face. 'I'll show you some of my pictures,' he said. 'I have to keep them hidden away, because my father can't bear me to want to be an artist!'

'Don't get up if you don't want to,' said Julian. 'I'll get them for you.'

'It's all right. If it's good for me to try and walk, I will,' said Martin, and got off the couch. He put his right foot gingerly to the floor and then stood up. 'Not so bad after all!' he said. He limped across the room to a bookcase. He put his hand behind the second row of books and brought out a cardboard case, big and flat. He took it to the table. He opened it and spread out some pictures.

'Gracious!' said Anne. 'They're *beautiful*! Did you really do these?'

They were queer pictures for a boy to draw, for they were of flowers and trees, birds and butterflies – all drawn and coloured most perfectly, every detail put in lovingly.

Julian looked at them in surprise. This boy was certainly gifted. Why, these drawings were as good as any he had ever seen in exhibitions! He picked a few up and took them to the window.

'Do you mean to say your father doesn't think these are good – doesn't think it's worth while to let you train as an artist?' he said, in surprise.

'He hates my pictures,' said Martin, bitterly. 'I ran away from school, and went to an art-school to train – but he found me and forbade me to think of drawing any more. He thinks it's a weak, feeble thing for a man to do. So I only do it in secret now.'

The children looked at Martin with sympathy. It seemed an awful thing to them that a boy who had no mother, should have a father who hated the thing his son most loved. No wonder he always looked dull and miserable and sullen!

'It's very bad luck,' said Julian at last. 'I wish we could do something to help.'

'Well – get me those figures and the paint tins from the coastguard,' said Martin, eagerly. 'Will you? Father won't be back till six. I'll have time to do them. And do stay and have tea with me. It's so dull up here. I hate it.'

'Yes, I'll get the things for you,' said Julian. 'I can't for the life of me see why you shouldn't have something to

amuse yourself with if you want to. And we'll ring up my aunt and tell her we're staying here to tea – so long as we don't eat everything you've got!'

'Oh, that's all right,' said Martin, looking very cheerful indeed. 'There's plenty of food in the house. My father has an enormous appetite. I say, thanks most awfully.'

Julian rang up his aunt. The girls and Dick went to fetch the figures and the paint from the coastguard. They brought them back and arranged them on a table beside

Martin. His eyes brightened at once. He seemed quite different.

'This is grand,' he said. 'Now I can get on! It's a silly little job, this, but it will help the old man next door, and I'm always happy when I'm messing about with a brush and paints!'

Martin was very, very clever at painting the little figures. He was quick and deft, and Anne sat watching him, quite fascinated. George went to hunt in the larder for the tea-things. There was certainly plenty of food! She cut some bread and butter, found some new honey, brought out a huge chocolate cake and some ginger buns, and put the kettle on to boil.

'I say, this is really grand,' said Martin again. 'I wish my father wasn't coming back till eight. By the way – where's the dog? I thought he always went everywhere with you! Where's Timmy?'

14

A shock for George

Dick looked at George. He didn't think it would matter telling Martin where Timmy was, so long as George didn't give the *reason* why he had been left on the island.

But George was going to hold her tongue now. She looked at Martin and spoke quite airily. 'Oh, Timmy? We left him behind today. He's all right.'

'Gone out shopping with your mother, I suppose, hoping for a visit to the butcher's!' said Martin. This was the first joke he had ever made to the children, and though it was rather a feeble one they laughed heartily. Martin looked pleased. He began to try and think of another little joke, while his deft hands put reds and blues and greens on the little wooden figures.

They all had a huge tea. Then, when the clock said a quarter to six the girls carried the painted figures carefully back to the coastguard, who was delighted with them. Dick took back the little tins of paint, and the brush stuck in a jar of turpentine.

'Well now, he's clever that boy, isn't he?' said the

coastguard, eyeing the figures in delight. 'Looks sort of miserable and sulky – but he's not a bad sort of boy!'

'I'll just have one more squint through your telescope,' said George, 'before it gets too dark.'

She tilted it towards her island. But once more there was no sign of Timmy, or of her father either. She looked for some time, and then went to join the others. She shook her head as they raised their eyebrows inquiringly.

The girls washed up the tea-things, and cleared away neatly. Nobody felt as if they wanted to wait and see Mr Curton. They didn't feel as if they liked him very much, now they knew how hard he was on Martin.

'Thanks for a lovely afternoon,' said Martin, limping to the door with them. 'I enjoyed my spot of painting, to say nothing of your company.'

'You stick out for your painting,' said Julian. 'If it's the thing you've *got* to do, and you know it, you must go all out for it. See?'

'Yes,' said Martin, and his face went sullen again. 'But there are things that make it difficult – things I can't very well tell you. Oh well – never mind! I dare say it will all come right one day, and I'll be a famous artist with pictures in the academy!'

'Come on, quickly,' said Dick, in a low voice to Julian. 'There's his father coming back!'

They hurried off down the cliff-path, seeing Mr Curton out of the corner of their eyes, coming up the other path.

'Horrid man!' said Anne. 'Forbidding Martin to do what he really longs to do. And he seemed so nice and jolly and all-over-us, didn't he?'

'Very all-over-us,' said Dick, smiling at Anne's new word. 'But there are a lot of people like that – one thing at home and quite another outside!'

'I hope Mr Curton hasn't been trying to explore that passage in the side of the quarry,' said George, looking back, and watching the man walk up to his back door. 'It would be too bad if he butted in and spoilt our fun. I mean – there may be nothing to discover at all – but it will be fun even finding there *is* nothing.'

'Very involved!' said Dick, with a grin. 'But I gather what you mean. I say, that was a good tea, wasn't it?'

'Yes,' said George, looking all round her in an absent-minded manner.

'What's up?' said Dick. 'What are you looking like that for?'

'Oh – how silly of me – I was just looking for Timmy,' said George. 'You know, I'm so used to him always being at my heels or somewhere near that I just can't get used to him not being here.'

'Yes, I feel a bit like that too,' said Julian. 'As if there was something missing all the time. Good old Tim! We shall miss him awfully, all of us – but you most of all, George.'

'Yes. Especially on my bed at night,' said George. 'I shan't be able to go to sleep for ages and ages.'

'I'll wrap a cushion up in a rug and plonk it down on your feet when you're in bed,' said Dick. 'Then it will feel like Timmy!'

'It won't! Don't be silly,' said George, rather crossly. 'And anyway it wouldn't *smell* like him. He's got a lovely smell.'

'Yes, a Timmy-smell,' agreed Anne. 'I like it too.'

The evening went very quickly, playing the endless game of monopoly again. Julian lay in bed later, watching for his uncle's signal. Needless to say, George was at the window too! They waited for half past ten.

'Now!' said Julian. And just as he spoke there came the first flash from the lantern in the tower.

'One,' counted George, 'two – three – four – five – six!' She waited anxiously to see if there were any more, but there weren't.

'Now you can go to bed in peace,' said Julian to George. 'Your father is all right, and that means that Timmy is all right too. Probably he has remembered to give Timmy a good supper and has had some himself as well!'

'Well, Timmy would soon remind him, if he forgot to feed him, that's one thing,' said George, slipping out of the room. 'Good night, Dick; good night, Ju! See you in the morning.'

And back she went to her own bed and snuggled down under the sheets. It was queer not to have Timmy on her feet. She tossed about for a while, missing him, and then fell asleep quite suddenly. She dreamed of her island. She was there with Timmy – and they were discovering ingots of gold down in the dungeon. What a lovely dream!

Next morning dawned bright and sunny again. The April sky was as blue as the forget-me-nots coming out in the garden. George gazed out of the dining-room window at breakfast time wondering if Timmy was running about her island.

'Dreaming about Tim?' said Julian, with a laugh. 'Never mind – you'll soon see him, George. Another hour or so and you'll feast your eyes on him through the coastguard's telescope!'

'Do you really think you'll be able to make out Tim, if he's in the tower with your father at half past ten?' asked her mother. 'I shouldn't have thought you would be able to.'

'Yes, I shall, Mother,' said George. 'It's a very powerful telescope, you know. I'll just go up and make my bed, then I'll go up the cliff-path. Anyone else coming?'

'I want Anne to help me with some turning out,' said her mother. 'I'm looking out some old clothes to give to the vicar's wife for her jumble sale. You don't mind helping me, Anne, do you?'

'No, I'd like to,' said Anne at once. 'What are the boys going to do?'

'I think I must do a bit of my holiday work this morning,' said Julian, with a sigh. 'I don't want to – but I've kept on putting it off. You'd better do some too, Dick. You know what you are – you'll leave it all to the last day if you're not careful!'

'All right. I'll do some too,' said Dick. 'You won't mind scooting up to the coastguard's cottage alone, will you, George?'

'Not a bit,' said George. 'I'll come back just after half past ten, as soon as I've spotted Timmy and Father.'

She disappeared to make her bed. Julian and Dick went to fetch some books. Anne went to make her bed too, and then came down to help her aunt. In a few minutes George yelled good-bye and rushed out of the house.

'What a hurricane!' said her mother. 'It seems as if George never walks if she can possibly run. Now Anne – put the clothes in three piles – the very old – the not so old – and the quite nice.'

Just before half past ten Julian went up to his window to watch for the signal from his uncle. He waited patiently. A few seconds after the half-hour the flashes came – one, two, three, four, five, six – good! Now George would settle down for the day. Perhaps they could go to the quarry in the afternoon. Julian went back to his books and was soon buried in them, with Dick grunting by his side.

At about five minutes to eleven there was the sound of running feet and panting breath. George appeared at the door of the sitting-room where the two boys were doing their work. They looked up.

George was red in the face, and her hair was wind-blown. She fought to get her breath enough to speak. 'Julian! Dick! Something's happened – Timmy wasn't there!'

'What do you mean?' said Julian in surprise. George slumped down on a chair, still panting. The boys could see that she was trembling too.

'It's serious, Julian! I tell you Timmy wasn't in the tower when the signals came!'

'Well – it only means that your absent-minded father forgot to take him up with him,' said Julian, in his most sensible voice. 'What *did* you see?'

'I had my eye glued to the telescope,' said George, 'and suddenly I saw someone come into the little glass room at the top. I looked for Timmy, of course, at once – but I tell you, he wasn't there! The six flashes came, the man disappeared – and that was all. No Timmy! Oh I do feel so dreadfully worried, Julian.'

'Well, don't be,' said Julian, soothingly. 'Honestly, I'm sure that's what happened. Your father forgot about Timmy. Anyway, if you saw *him*, obviously things are all right.'

'I'm not thinking about Father!' cried George. 'He must be all right if he flashed his signals – I'm thinking about Timmy. Why, even if Father forgot to take him, he'd go with him. You know that!'

'Your father might have shut the door at the bottom and prevented Timmy from going up,' said Dick.

'He might,' said George, frowning. She hadn't thought of that. 'Oh dear – now I shall worry all day long. *Why* didn't I stay with Timmy? What shall I do now?'

'Wait till tomorrow morning,' said Dick. 'Then probably you'll see old Tim all right.'

'Tomorrow morning! Why, that's *ages* away!' said poor George. She put her head in her hands and groaned. 'Oh, nobody understands how much I love Timmy. You would perhaps if you had a dog of your own, Julian. It's an awful feeling, really. Oh Timmy, are you all right?'

'Of course he's all right,' said Julian, impatiently. 'Do pull yourself together, George.'

'I *feel* as if something's wrong,' said George, looking obstinate. 'Julian – I think I'd better go across to the island.'

'No,' said Julian at once. 'Don't be idiotic, George. Nothing is wrong, except that your father's been forgetful. He's sent his OK signal. That's enough! You're not to go and create a scene over there with him. That would be disgraceful!'

'Well – I'll try and be patient,' said George, unexpectedly meek. She got up, looking worried. Julian spoke in a kinder voice.

'Cheer up, old thing! You do like to go off the deep end, don't you?'

15

In the middle of the night

George did not moan any more about her worries. She went about with an anxious look in her blue eyes, but she had the sense not to tell her mother how worried she was at not seeing Timmy in the glass room, when her father signalled.

She mentioned it, of course, but her mother took the same view as Julian did. 'There! I knew he'd forget to take Timmy up! He's so very forgetful when he's at work.'

The children decided to go to the quarry that afternoon and explore the tunnel under the shelf of rock. So they set off after their lunch. But when they came to the quarry, they did not dare to climb down the steep sides. The heavy rain of the day before had made them far too dangerous.

'Look,' said Julian, pointing to where the bushes and smaller plants were ripped up and crushed. 'I bet that's where old Martin fell down yesterday! He might have broken his neck!'

'Yes. I vote we don't attempt to go down till it's as dry as it was the other day,' said Dick.

It was very disappointing. They had brought torches, and a rope, and had looked forward to a little excitement. 'Well, what shall we do?' asked Julian.

'I'm going back home,' said George, unexpectedly. 'I'm tired. You others go for a walk.'

Anne looked at George. She did seem rather pale. 'I'll come back with you, George,' said Anne slipping her hand through her cousin's arm. But George shook it off.

'No thanks, Anne. I want to be alone.'

'Well – we'll go over to the cliff then,' said George. 'It'll be nice and blowy up there. See you later, George!'

They went off. George turned and sped back to Kirrin Cottage. Her mother was out. Joanna was upstairs in her bedroom. George went to the larder and took several things from it. She bundled them into a bag and then fled out of the house.

She found James the fisher-boy. 'James! You're not to tell a soul. I'm going over to Kirrin Island tonight – because I'm worried about Timmy. We left him there. Have my boat ready at ten o'clock.'

James was always ready to do anything in the world for George. He nodded and asked no questions at all. 'Right, Miss. It'll be ready. Anything you want put in it?'

'Yes, this bag,' said George. 'Now don't split on me, James. I'll be back tomorrow if I find Tim's all right.'

She fled back to the house. She hoped Joanna would not notice the things she had taken from the larder shelf.

'I can't help it if what I'm doing is wrong,' she kept whispering to herself. 'I know something isn't right with Timmy. And I'm not at all sure about Father, either. He *wouldn't* have forgotten his solemn promise to me about taking Timmy up with him. I'll have to go across to the island. I can't help it if it's wrong!'

The others wondered what was up with George when they came back from their walk. She was so fidgety and restless. They had tea and then did some gardening for

Aunt Fanny. George did some too, but her thoughts were far away, and twice her mother had to stop her pulling up seedlings instead of weeds.

Bedtime came. The girls got into bed at about a quarter to ten. Anne was tired and fell asleep at once. As soon as George heard her regular breathing she crept quietly out of bed and dressed again. She pulled on her warmest jersey, got her raincoat, rubber boots and a thick rug, and tiptoed downstairs.

Out of the side door she went and into the night. There was a bit of a moon in the sky, so it was not as dark as usual. George was glad. She would be able to see her way through the rocks a little now – though she was sure she could guide the boat even in the dark!

James was waiting for her. Her boat was ready. 'Everything's in,' said James. 'I'll push off. Now you be careful, Miss – and if you do scrape a rock, row like anything in case she fills and sinks. Ready?'

Off went George, hearing the lap-lap of the water against the sides of the boat. She heaved a sigh of relief, and began to row strongly away from the shore. She frowned as she rowed. Had she brought everything she might want? Two torches. Plenty of food. A tin-opener. Something to drink. A rug to wrap herself in tonight.

Back at Kirrin Cottage Julian lay in bed watching for his uncle's signal. Half past ten. Now for the signal. Ah, here they were! One – two – three – four – five – six! Good. Six and no more!

He wondered why George hadn't come into his and Dick's room to watch for them. She had last night. He got up, padded to the door of George's room and put his head in 'George!' he said softly. 'It's OK. Your father's signals have just come again.'

There was no reply. Julian heard regular breathing and turned to go back to bed. The girls must be asleep already! Well, George couldn't really be worrying much about

Timmy now, then! Julian got into his bed and soon fell asleep himself. He had no idea that George's bed was empty – no idea that even now George was battling with the waves that guarded Kirrin Island!

It was more difficult than she had expected, for the moon did not really give very much light, and had an annoying way of going behind a cloud just when she badly needed every scrap of light she could get. But, deftly and cleverly, she managed to make her way through the passage between the hidden rocks. Thank goodness the tide was high so that most of them were well below the surface!

At last she swung her boat into the little cove. Here the water was perfectly calm. Panting a little, George pulled her boat up as far as she could. Then she stood in the darkness and thought hard.

What was she going to do? She did not know where her father's hiding-place was – but she felt certain the entrance to it must be somewhere in or near the little stone room. Should she make her way to that?

Yes, she would. It would be the only place to shelter in for the night, anyway. She would put on her torch when she got there, and hunt round for any likely entrance to the hiding-place. If she found it, she would go in – and what a surprise she would give her father! If old Timmy was there he would go mad with delight.

She took the heavy bag, draped the rug over her arm, and set off. She did not dare to put on her torch yet, in case the unknown enemy was lurking near. After all, her father had heard him cough at night!

George was not frightened. She did not even think about being frightened. All her thoughts were set on finding Timmy and making sure he was safe.

She came to the little stone room. It was pitch-dark in there, of course – not even the faint light of the moon pierced into its blackness. George had to put on her torch.

She put down her bundle by the wall at the back, near the old fireplace recess. She draped the rug over it and sat down to have a rest, switching off her torch.

After a while she got up cautiously and switched on her torch again. She began to search for the hiding-place. Where *could* the entrance be? She flashed her torch on to every flagstone in the floor of the room. But not one looked as if it had been moved or lifted. There was nothing to show where there might be an entrance underground.

She moved round the walls, examining those too in the light of her torch. No – there was no sign that a hidden way lay behind any of those stones either. It was most tantalising. If she only knew!

She went to wrap the rug round her, and to sit and think. It was cold now. She was shivering, as she sat there in the dark, trying to puzzle out where the hidden entrance could be.

And then she heard a sound! She jumped and then stiffened all over, holding her breath painfully. What was it?

There was a curious grating noise. Then a slight thud. It came from the recess where people long ago had built their big log fires! George sat perfectly still, straining her eyes and ears.

She saw a beam of light in the fireplace recess. Then she heard a man's cough!

Was it her father? He had a cough at times. She listened hard. The beam of light grew brighter. Then she heard another noise – it sounded as if someone had jumped down from somewhere! And then – a voice!

'Come on!'

It was not her father's voice! George grew cold with fear then. Not her father's voice! Then what had happened to him – and to Timmy?

Someone else jumped down into the recess, grumbling. 'I'm not used to this crawling about!'

That wasn't her father's voice either. So there were *two* unknown enemies! Not one. And they knew her father's secret workroom. George felt almost faint with horror. Whatever had happened to him and Timmy?

The men walked out of the little stone room without seeing George at all. She guessed they were going to the tower. How long would they be? Long enough for her to search for the place they had appeared from?

She strained her ears again. She heard their footsteps

going into the great yard. She tiptoed to the doorway and looked out. Yes – there was the light of their torch near the tower! If they were going up, there would be plenty of time to look round.

She went back into the little stone room. Her hands were trembling and she found it difficult to switch on her torch. She went to the fireplace recess and flashed the light in it.

She gave a gasp! Half way up the recess at the back was a black opening! She flashed the light up there. Evidently there was a movable stone half way up that swung back and revealed an entrance behind. An entrance to what? Were there steps such as were shown in the old map?

Feeling quite breathless, George stood on tip-toe and flashed her light into the hole. Yes – there were steps! They went down into the wall at the back. She remembered that the little stone room backed on to one of the immensely thick old walls still left.

She stood there, uncertain what to do. Had she better go down and see if she could find Timmy and her father? But if she did, she might be made a prisoner too. On the other hand, if she stayed outside, and the men came back and shut up the entrance, she might not be able to open it. She would be worse off than ever!

'I'll go down!' she suddenly decided. 'But I'd better take my bag and the rug, in case the men come back and see them. I don't want them to know I'm on the island if I can help it! I could hide them somewhere down there, I expect. I wonder if this entrance leads to the dungeons.'

She lifted up the rug and the bag and pushed them into the hole. She heard the bag roll down the steps, the tins inside making a muffled noise.

Then she climbed up herself. Gracious, what a long dark flight of steps! Wherever did they lead to?

16

Down to the caves

George went cautiously down the stone steps. They were steep and narrow. 'I should think they run right down in the middle of the stone wall,' thought George 'Goodness, here's a narrow bit!'

It was so narrow that she had to go sideways. 'A fat man would never get through there!' she thought to herself. 'Hallo – the steps have ended!'

She had got the rug round her shoulders, and had picked up her bag on the way down. In her other hand she held her torch. It was terribly dark and quiet down there. George did not feel scared because she was hoping to see Timmy at any moment. No one could feel afraid with Timmy just round the corner, ready to welcome them!

She stood at the bottom of the steps, her torch showing her a narrow tunnel. It curved sharply to the left. 'Now will it join the dungeons from here?' she wondered, trying to get her sense of direction to help her. 'They can't be far off. But there's no sign of them at the moment.'

She went down the narrow tunnel. Once the roof came

down so low she almost had to crawl. She flashed her torch on it. She saw black rock there, which had evidently been too hard to be removed by the tunnel-builders long ago.

The tunnel went on and on and on. George was puzzled. Surely by now she must have gone by all the dungeons! Why – she must be heading towards the shore of the island! How very queer! Didn't this tunnel join the dungeons then? A little further and she would be under the bed of the sea itself.

The tunnel took a deep slope downwards. More steps appeared, cut roughly from rock. George climbed down them cautiously. Where in the world was she going?

At the bottom of the steps the tunnel seemed to be cut out of solid rock – or else it was a natural passage, not made by man at all. George didn't know. Her torch showed her black, rocky walls and roof, and her feet stumbled over an irregular rocky path. How she longed for Timmy beside her!

'I must be very deep down,' she thought, pausing to flash her torch round her once more. 'Very deep down and very far from the castle! Good gracious – whatever's that awful noise?'

She listened. She heard a muffled booming and moaning. Was it her father doing one of his experiments? The noise went on and on, a deep, never-ending boom.

'Why – I believe it's the sea!' said George, amazed. She stood and listened again. 'Yes – it *is* the sea – over my head! I'm under the rocky bed of Kirrin Bay!'

And now poor George did feel a bit scared! She thought of the great waves surging above her, she thought of the restless, moving water scouring the rocky bed over her head, and felt frightened in case the sea should find a way to leak down into her narrow tunnel!

'Now don't be silly,' she told herself sternly. 'This tunnel has been here under the sea-bed for hundreds of years – why should it suddenly become unsafe just when *you* are in it, George?'

Talking to herself like this, to keep up her spirits, she went on again. It was very queer indeed to think she was walking under the sea. So this was where her father was at work! Under the sea itself.

And then George suddenly remembered something he had said to them all, the first time they had visited him on the island. What was it now? 'Oh yes! He said he had to have water *above* and *around* him!' said George. '*Now* I see what he meant! His workroom is somewhere down here – so the sea-water is *above* him – and it's all *round* the tower, because it's built on an island!'

Water above and water around – so that was why her father had chosen Kirrin Island for his experiment. How had he found the secret passage under the sea, though? 'Why, even I didn't know of that,' said George. 'Hallo – what am I coming to?'

She stopped. The passage had suddenly widened out into an enormous dark cave, whose roof was unexpectedly high, lost in dark shadows. George stared round. She saw queer things there that she didn't understand at all – wires, glass boxes, little machines that seemed to be at work without a sound, whose centres were alive with queer, gleaming, shivering light.

Sudden sparks shot up now and again, and when that happened a funny smell crept round the cave. 'How weird all this is!' thought George. 'However can Father understand all these machines and things! I wonder where he is. I do hope those men haven't made him prisoner somewhere!'

From this queer Aladdin's cave another tunnel led. George switched on her torch again and went into it. It was much like the other one, but the roof was higher.

She came to another cave, smaller this time, and crammed with wires of all kinds. There was a curious humming

sound here, like thousands of bees in a hive. George half-expected to see some flying round.

'It must be these wires making the noise,' she said. There was nobody in the cave at all, but it led into another one, and George hoped that soon she would find Timmy and her father.

She went into the next cave, which was perfectly empty and very cold. She shivered. Then down another passage, and into a small cave. The first thing she saw beyond this tiny cave was a light!

A light! Then perhaps she was coming to the cave her father must be in! She flashed her torch round the little cave she was now standing in and saw tins of food, bottles of beer, tins of sweets, and a pile of clothes of some sort. Ah, this was where her father kept his stores. She went on to the next cave. wondering why Timmy had not heard her and come to greet her.

She looked cautiously into the cave where the light came from. Sitting at a table, his head in his hands, perfectly still, was her father! There was no sign of Timmy.

'Father!' said George. The man at the table jumped violently and turned round. He stared at George as if he really could not believe his eyes. Then he turned back again, and buried his face in his hands.

'*Father*!' said George again, quite frightened because he did not say anything to her.

He looked round again, and this time he got up. He stared at George once more, and then sat down heavily. George ran to him. 'What's the matter? Oh Father, what's the matter? Where's Timmy?'

'George! Is it *really* you, George? I thought I must be dreaming when I looked up and saw you!' said her father. 'How did you get here? Good gracious, it's impossible that you should be here!'

'Father are you all right? What's happened – and where's Timmy?' said George, urgently. She looked all round, but could see no sign of him. Her heart went cold. Surely nothing awful had happened to Timmy?

'Did you see two men?' asked her father. 'Where were they?'

'Oh Father – we keep asking each other questions and

not answering them!' said George. 'Tell me first – where is Timmy?'

'I don't know,' said her father. 'Did those two men go to the tower?'

'Yes,' said George. 'Father, what's happened?'

'Well, if they've gone to the tower, we've got about an hour in peace,' said her father. 'Now listen to me, George, very carefully. This is terribly important.'

'I'm listening,' said George. 'But do hurry up and tell me about Timmy.'

'These two men were parachuted down on to the island, to try and find out my secret,' said her father. 'I'll tell you what my experiments are for, George – they are to find a way of replacing all coal, coke and oil – an idea to give the world all the heat and power it wants, and to do away with mines and miners.'

'Good gracious!' said George. 'It would be one of the most wonderful things the world has ever known.'

'Yes,' said her father. 'And I should *give* it to the whole world – it shall not be in the power of any one country, or collection of men. It shall be a gift to the whole of mankind – but, George, there are men who want my secret for themselves, so that they may make colossal fortunes out of it.'

'How hateful!' cried George. 'Go on, Father – how did they hear of it?'

'Well, I was at work on this idea with some of my colleagues, my fellow-workers,' said her father. 'And one of them betrayed us, and went to some powerful business men to tell them of my idea. So when I knew this I decided to come away in secret and finish my experiments by myself. Then nobody could betray me.'

'And you came here!' said George. 'To my island.'

'Yes – because I needed water over me and water around me,' said her father. 'Quite by chance I looked at a copy of that old map, and thought that if the passage shown there – the one leading from the little stone room, I mean – if the passage there *really* did lead under the sea, as it seemed to show, that would be the ideal place to finish my experiments.'

'Oh Father – and I made such a fuss!' said George, ashamed now, to remember how cross she had been.

'Did you?' said her father, as if he had forgotten all about that. 'Well, I got all my stuff and came here. And now these fellows have found me, and got hold of me!'

'Poor Father! Can't I help?' said George. 'I could go back and bring help over here, couldn't I?'

'Yes, you could!' said her father. 'But you mustn't let those men see you, George.'

'I'll do anything you want me to, Father, anything!' said George. 'But first do tell me what's happened to Timmy?'

116

'Well, he kept by me all the time,' said her father. 'Really, he's a wonderful dog, George. And then, this morning, just as I was coming out of the entrance in that little room to go up into the tower with Timmy to signal, the two men pounced on me and forced me back here.'

'But what happened to Timmy?' asked George, impatiently. Would her father *never* tell her what she wanted to know?

'He flew at the men, of course,' said her father. 'But somehow or other one of them lassoed him with a noose of rope and caught him. They pulled the rope so right round his neck that he almost choked.'

'Oh poor, poor Timmy,' said George, and the tears ran down her cheeks. 'Is he – do you think – he's all right, Father?'

'Yes. From what I heard the men saying afterwards I think they've taken him to some cave and shut him in there,' said her father. 'Anyway, I saw one of them getting some dog-biscuits out of a bag this evening – so that looks as if he's alive and kicking – and hungry!'

George heaved a great sigh of relief. So long as Timmy was alive and all right! She took a few steps towards what she thought must be another cave. 'I'm going to find Timmy, Father,' she said. 'I *must* find him!'

17

Timmy at last

'No, George!' called her father sharply. 'Come back. There is something very important I want to say. Come here!'

George went over to him, filled with impatience to get to Timmy, wherever he was. She *must* find him!

'Now listen,' said her father. 'I have a book in which I have made all my notes of this great experiment. The men haven't found it! I want you to take it safely to the mainland, George. Don't let it out of your sight! If the men get hold of it they would have all the information they needed!'

'But don't they know everything just by looking at your wires and machines and things?' asked George.

'They know a very great deal,' said her father, 'and they've found out a lot more since they've been here – but not quite enough. I daren't destroy my book of notes, because if anything should happen to me, my great idea would be completely lost. So, George, I must entrust it to you and you must take it to an address I will give you, and hand it to the person there.'

'It's an awful responsibility,' said George, a little scared of handling a book which meant so much, not only to her father, but possibly to the whole of the world. 'But I'll do my best, Father. I'll hide in one of the caves till the men come back, and then I'll slip back up the passage to the hidden entrance, get out, go to my boat and row back to the mainland. Then I'll deliver your book of notes without fail, and get help sent over here to you.'

'Good girl,' said her father, and gave her a hug. 'Honestly, George, you do behave as bravely as any boy. I'm proud of you.'

George thought that was the nicest thing her father had ever said to her. She smiled at him. 'Well, Father, I'll go and see if I can find Timmy now. I simply must see that he's all right before I go to hide in one of the other caves.'

'Very well,' said her father. 'The man who took the biscuits went in that direction – still further under the sea, George. Oh – by the way – how is it you're here, in the middle of the night?'

It seemed to strike her father for the first time that George also might have a story to tell. But George felt that she really couldn't waste any more time – she *must* find Timmy!

'I'll tell you later, Father,' she said. 'Oh – where's that book of notes?'

Her father rose and went to the back of the cave. He took a box and stood on it. He ran his hand along a dark ridge of rock, and felt about until he had found what he wanted.

He brought down a slim book, whose pages were of very thin paper. He opened the book and George saw many beautifully drawn diagrams, and pages of notes in her father's small neat handwriting.

'Here you are,' said her father, handing her the book, 'do

119

the best you can. If anything happens to me, this book will still enable my fellow-workers to give my idea to the world. If I come through this all right, I shall be glad to have the book, because it will mean I shall not have to work out all my experiments again.'

George took the precious book. She stuffed it into her macintosh pocket, which was a big one. 'I'll keep it safe, Father. Now I must go and find Timmy, or those two men will be back before I can hide in one of the other caves.'

She left her father's cave and went into the next one. There was nothing there at all. Then on she went down a passage that twisted and turned in the rock.

And then she heard a sound she longed to hear. A whine! Yes, really a whine!

'Timmy!' shouted George, eagerly. 'Oh Timmy! I'm coming!'

Timmy's whine stopped suddenly. Then he barked joyously. 'Woof, woof, woof, woof!' George almost fell as she tried to run down the narrow tunnel. Her torch showed her a big boulder that seemed to be blocking up a small cave in the side of the tunnel. Behind the boulder Timmy barked, and scraped frantically!

George tugged at the stone with all her strength. 'Timmy!' she panted. 'Timmy! I'll get you out! I'm coming! Oh, Timmy!'

The stone moved a little. George tugged again. It was almost too heavy for her to move at all, but despair made her stronger than she had ever been in her life. The stone quite suddenly swung to one side, and George just got one of her feet out of its way in time, or it would have been crushed.

Timmy squeezed out of the space left. He flung himself on George, who fell on the ground with her arms tight round him. He licked her face and whined, and she buried her nose in his thick fur in joy. 'Timmy! What have they done to you? Timmy, I came as soon as I could!'

120

Timmy whined again and again in joy, and tried to paw and lick George as if he couldn't have enough of her. It would have been difficult to say which of the two was the happier.

At last George pushed Timmy away firmly. 'Timmy we've got work to do! We've got to escape from here and get across to the mainland and bring help.'

'Woof,' said Timmy. George stood up and flashed her torch into the tiny cave where Timmy had been. She saw that there was a bowl of water there and some biscuits. The men had not ill-treated him, then, except to lasso him and half-choke him when they caught him. She felt round his neck tenderly, but except for a swollen ridge there, he seemed none the worse.

'Now hurry up – we'll go back to Father's cave – and then find another cave beyond his to hide in till the two men come back from the tower. Then we'll creep out into the little stone room and row back to the mainland,' said George. 'I've got a very, very important book here in my pocket, Timmy.'

Timmy growled suddenly, and the hairs on the back of his neck rose up. George stiffened, and stood listening.

A stern voice came down the passage. 'I don't know who you are or where you've come from – but if you have dared to let that dog loose he'll be shot! And, to show you that I mean what I say, here's something to let you know I've a revolver!'

Then there came a deafening crash, as the man pulled the trigger, and a bullet hit the roof somewhere in the passage. Timmy and George almost jumped out of their skins. Timmy would have leapt up the passage at once, but George had her hand on his collar. She was very frightened, and tried hard to think what was best to do.

The echoes of the shot went on and on. It was horrid. Timmy stopped growling, and George stayed absolutely still.

'Well?' said the voice, 'did you hear what I said? If that dog is loose, he'll be shot. I'm not having my plans spoilt now. And you, whoever you are, will please come up the tunnel and let me see you. But I warn you – if the dog's with you, that's the end of him!'

'Timmy! Timmy, run away and hide somewhere!' whispered George suddenly. And then she remembered something else that filled her with despair. She had her father's precious book of notes with her – in her pocket! Suppose the man found it on her? It would break her

father's heart to know that his wonderful secret had been stolen from him after all.

George hurriedly took the thin, flat little book from her pocket. She pushed it at Timmy. 'Put it in your mouth. Take it with you, Tim. And go and hide till it's safe to come. Quick! Go, Timmy, go! I'll be all right.'

To her great relief Timmy, with the book in his mouth, turned and disappeared down the tunnel that led further under the sea. How she hoped he would find a safe hiding place! The tunnel must end soon – but maybe before it did, Timmy would settle down in some dark corner and wait for her to call him again.

'Will you come up the passage or not?' shouted the voice angrily. 'You'll be sorry if I have to come and fetch you – because I shall shoot all the way along!' 'I'm coming!' called George, in a small voice, and she went up the passage. She soon saw a beam of light, and in a moment she was in the flash of a powerful torch. There was a surprised exclamation.

'Good heavens! A boy! What are *you* doing here, and where did you come from?'

George's short curly hair made the man with the torch think she was a boy, and George did not tell him he was wrong. The man held a revolver, but he let it drop as he saw George.

'I only came to rescue my dog, and to find my father,' said George, in a meek voice.

'Well, you can't move that heavy stone!' said the man. 'A kid like you wouldn't have the strength. And you can't rescue your father either! We've got him prisoner, as you no doubt saw.'

'Yes,' said George, delighted to think that the man was sure she had not been strong enough to move the big stone. She wasn't going to say a word about Timmy! If the man thought he was still shut up in that tiny cave, well and good!

123

Then she heard her father's voice, anxiously calling from somewhere beyond the man. 'George! Is that you? Are you all right?'

'Yes, Father!' shouted back George, hoping that he would not ask anything about Timmy. The man beckoned her to come to him. Then he pushed her in front of him and they walked to her father's cave.

'I've brought your boy back,' said the man. 'Silly little idiot – thinking he could set that savage dog free! We've got him penned up in a cave with a big boulder in front!'

Another man came in from the opposite end of the cave. He was amazed to see George. The other man explained.

'When I got down here, I heard a noise out beyond this cave, the dog barking and someone talking to him – and found this kid there, trying to set the dog free. I'd have shot the dog, of course, if he *had* been freed.'

'But – how did this boy get here?' asked the other man, still amazed.

'Maybe *he* can tell us that!' said the other. And then, for the first time, George's father heard how George had got there and why.

She told them how she had watched for Timmy in the glass room of the tower and hadn't seen him – and that had worried her and made her suspicious. So she had come across to the island in her boat at night, and had seen where the men came from. She had gone down the tunnel, and kept on till she came to the cave, where she had found her father.

The three men listened in silence. 'Well, you're a tiresome nuisance,' one of the men said to George, 'but my word, you're a son to be proud of. It's not many boys would have been brave enough to run so much risk for anyone.'

'Yes. I'm really proud of you, George,' said her father. He looked at her anxiously. She knew what he was thinking – what about his precious book? Had she been sensible enough to hide it? She did not dare to let him know anything while the men were there.

'Now, this complicates matters,' said the other man, looking at George. 'If you don't go back home you'll soon be missed, and there will be all kinds of search-parties going on – and maybe someone will send over to the island here to tell your father you have disappeared! We don't want anyone here at present – not till we know what we want to know!'

He turned to George's father. 'If you will tell us what we want to know, and give us all your notes, we will set you free, give you whatever sum of money you ask us for, and disappear ourselves.'

'And if I still say I won't?' said George's father.

'Then I am afraid we shall blow up the whole of your machines and the tower – and possibly you will never be found again because you will be buried down here,' said the man, in a voice that was suddenly very hard.

There was a dead silence. George looked at her father. 'You couldn't do a thing like that,' he said at last. 'You would gain nothing by it at all!'

'It's all or nothing with us,' said the man. 'All or nothing. Make up your mind. We'll give you till half past ten tomorrow morning – about seven hours. Then either you tell us everything, or we blow the island sky-high!'

They went out of the cave and left George and her father together. Only seven hours! And then, perhaps, the end of Kirrin Island!

18

Half past four in the morning

As soon as the men were out of earshot, George's father spoke in a low voice.

'It's no good. I'll have to let them have my book of notes. I can't risk having you buried down here, George. I don't mind anything for myself – workers of my sort have to be ready to take risks all their lives – but it's different now you're here!'

'Father, I haven't got the book of notes,' whispered George, thankfully. 'I gave them to Timmy. I *did* manage to get that stone away from the entrance to his little prison – though the men think I didn't! I gave the book to Timmy and told him to go and hide till I fetched him.'

'Fine work, George!' said her father. 'Well – perhaps if you got Timmy now and brought him here – he could deal with these two men before they suspect he is free! He is quite capable of getting them both down on the ground at once.'

'Oh yes! It's your only chance,' said George. 'I'll go and get him now. I'll go a little way along the passage and whistle. Father – why didn't *you* go and try and rescue Timmy?'

'I didn't want to leave my book,' said her father. 'I dared not take it with me, in case the men came after me and found it. They've been looking in all the caves for it. I couldn't bear to leave it here, and go and look for the dog. I was sure he was all right, when I saw the men taking biscuits out of the bag. Now do go, George, and whistle to Timmy. The men may be back at any moment.'

George took her torch and went into the passage that led to the little cave where Timmy had been. She whistled loudly, and then waited. But no Timmy came. She whistled again, and then went farther along the passage. Still no Timmy.

She called him loudly. 'TIMMY! TIMMY! COME HERE!' But Timmy did not come. There was no sound of scampering feet, no joyful bark.

'Oh bother!' thought George. 'I hope he hasn't gone so far away that he can't hear me. I'll go a little farther.'

So she made her way along the tunnel, past the cave where Timmy had been, and then on down the tunnel again. Still no Timmy.

George rounded a corner and then saw that the tunnel split into three. Three different passages, all dark, silent and cold. Oh dear! She didn't in the least know which to take. She took the one on the left.

But that also split into three a little way on! George stopped. 'I shall get absolutely lost in this maze of passages under the sea if I go on,' she thought. 'I simply daren't. It's too frightening. TIMMY! TIMMY!'

Her voice went echoing along the passage and sounded very queer indeed. She retraced her steps and went right back to her father's cave, feeling miserable.

'Father, there's no sign of Timmy at all. He must have

gone along one of the passages and got lost! Oh dear, this is awful. There are lots of tunnels beyond this cave. It seems as if the whole rocky bed of the sea is mined with tunnels!' George sat down and looked very downhearted.

'Quite likely,' said her father. 'Well – that's a perfectly good plan gone wrong. We must try and think of another.'

'I do wonder what Julian and the others will think when they wake up and find me gone,' said George, suddenly. 'They might even come and try to find me here.'

'That wouldn't be much good,' said her father. 'These men will simply come down here and wait, and nobody will know where we are. The others don't know of the entrance in the little stone room, do they?'

'No,' said George. 'If they came over here I'm sure they'd never find it! We've looked before. And that would mean they'd be blown up with the island. Father, this is simply dreadful.'

'If only we knew where Timmy was!' said her father, 'or if we could get a message to Julian to tell him not to come. What's the time? My word, it's half past three in the early morning! I suppose Julian and the others are fast asleep.'

Julian *was* fast asleep. So was Anne. Dick was in a deep sleep as well, so nobody guessed that George's bed was empty.

But, about half past four Anne awoke, feeling very hot. 'I really must open the window!' she thought. 'I'm boiling!'

She got up and went to the window. She opened it, and stood looking out. The stars were out and the bay shone faintly.

'George,' whispered Anne. 'Are you awake?'

She listened for a reply. But none came. Then she listened more intently. Why, she couldn't even hear George's breathing! Surely George was there?

She felt over George's bed. It was flat and empty. She

switched on the light and looked at it. George's pyjamas were still on the bed. Her clothes were gone.

'George has gone to the island!' said Anne, in a fright. 'All in the dark by herself!'

She went to the boys' room. She felt about Julian's bed for his shoulder, and shook him hard. He woke up with a jump. 'What is it? What's up?'

'Julian! George is gone. Her bed's not been slept in,' whispered Anne. Her whisper awoke Dick, and soon both boys were sitting up wide awake.

'Blow! I might have guessed she'd do a fool thing like that,' said Julian. 'In the middle of the night too – and all those dangerous rocks to row round. *Now* what are we going to do about it? I *told* her she wasn't to go to the island – Timmy would be quite all right! I expect Uncle Quentin forgot to take him up to the tower with him yesterday, that's all. She might have waited till half past ten this morning – then she would probably have seen him.'

'Well – we can't do anything now, I suppose, can we?' said Anne, anxiously.

'Not a thing,' said Julian. 'I've no doubt she's safely on Kirrin Island by now, making a fuss of Timmy, and having a good old row with Uncle Quentin. Really George is the limit!'

They talked for half an hour and then Julian looked at his watch. 'Five o'clock. We'd better try and get a bit more sleep. Aunt Fanny will be worried in the morning when she hears of George's latest escapade!'

Anne went back to her room. She got into bed and fell asleep. Julian could not sleep – he kept thinking of George and wondering where exactly she was. Wouldn't he give her a talking-to when she came back!

He suddenly heard a peculiar noise downstairs. Whatever could it be? It sounded like someone climbing in at a window. Was there one open? Yes, the window of the little wash-place might be open. Crash! What in the world was that? It couldn't be a burglar – no burglar would be foolish enough to make such a noise.

There was a sound on the stairs, and then the bedroom door was pushed open. In alarm Julian put out his hand to switch on the light, but before he could do something heavy jumped right on top of him!

He yelled and Dick woke up with a jump. He put on the light – then Julian saw what was on his bed – Timmy!

'Timmy! How did you get here? Where's George! Timmy, is it really you?'

'Timmy!' echoed Dick, amazed. 'Has George brought him back then? Is she here too?'

Anne came in, wakened by the noise. 'Why, *Timmy*! Oh Julian, is George back too, then?'

'No, apparently not,' said Julian, puzzled. 'I say, Tim, what's this you've got in your mouth? Drop it, old chap, drop it!'

Timmy dropped it. Julian picked it up from the bed. 'It's a book of notes – all in Uncle's handwriting! What *does* this mean? How did Timmy get hold of it – and why did he bring it here? It's most extraordinary!'

Nobody could imagine why Timmy had suddenly appeared with the book of notes – and no George.

'It's very queer,' said Julian. 'There's something I don't understand here. Let's go and wake Aunt Fanny.'

So they went and woke her up, telling her all they knew. She was very worried indeed to hear that George was gone. She picked up the book of notes and knew at once that it was very important.

'I must put this into the safe,' she said. 'I know this is valuable. How *did* Timmy get hold of it?'

Timmy was acting queerly. He kept pawing at Julian and whining. He had been very pleased to see everyone, but he seemed to have something on his mind.

'What is it, old boy?' asked Dick. 'How did you get here? You didn't swim, because you're not wet. If you came in a boat, it must have been with George – and yet you've left her behind!'

'*I* think something's happened to George,' said Anne, suddenly. 'I think Timmy keeps pawing you to tell you to go with him and find her. Perhaps she brought him back in the boat, and then was terribly tired and fell asleep on the beach or something. We ought to go and see.'

'Yes, I think we ought,' said Julian. 'Aunt Fanny, would you like to wake Joanna and get something hot ready, in case we find George is tired out and cold? We'll go down to the beach and look. It will soon be daylight now. The eastern sky is just beginning to show its first light.'

'Well go and dress then,' said Aunt Fanny, still looking very worried indeed. 'Oh, what a dreadful family I've got – always in some scrape or other!'

The three children began to dress. Timmy watched them, waiting patiently till they were ready. Then they all went downstairs and out of doors. Julian turned towards the beach, but Timmy stood still. He pawed at Dick and then ran a few steps in the opposite direction.

'Why – he doesn't *want* us to go the beach! He wants us to go another way!' cried Julian, in surprise. 'All right, Timmy – you lead the way and we'll follow!'

19

A meeting with Martin

Timmy ran round the house and made for the moor behind. It was most extraordinary. Wherever was he going?

'This is awfully queer,' said Julian. 'I'm sure George can't be anywhere in this direction.'

Timmy went on swiftly, occasionally turning his head to make sure everyone was following him. He led the way to the quarry!

'The quarry! Did George come here then?' said Dick. 'But why?'

The dog disappeared down into the middle of the quarry, slipping and sliding down the steep sides as he went. The others followed as best they could. Luckily it was not as slippery as before, and they reached the bottom without accident.

Timmy went straight to the shelf of rock and disappeared underneath it. They heard him give a short sharp bark as if to say 'Come on! This is the way! Hurry up!'

'He's gone into the tunnel under there,' said Dick. 'Where we thought we might explore and didn't. There must be a passage or something there, then. But is George there?'

'I'll go first,' said Julian, and wriggled through the hole. He was soon in the wider bit and then came out into the part where he could almost stand. He walked a little way in the dark, hearing Timmy bark impatiently now and then. But in a moment or two Julian stopped.

'It's no good trying to follow you in the dark, Timmy!' he called. 'We'll have to go back and get torches. I can't see a foot in front of me!'

Dick was just wriggling through the first part of the hole. Julian called to him to go back.

'It's too dark,' he said. 'We must go and get torches. If George for some reason is up this passage, she must have had an accident, and we'd better get a rope, and some brandy.'

Anne began to cry. She didn't like the idea of George lying hurt in that dark passage. Julian put his arm round her as soon as he was in the open air again. He helped her up the sides of the quarry, followed by Dick.

'Now don't worry. We'll get her all right. But it beats me why she went there – and I still can't imagine how Tim and she came from the island, if they are here, instead of on the beach!'

'Look – there's Martin!' suddenly said Dick in surprise. So there was! He was standing at the top of the quarry, and seemed just as surprised to see them as they were to see him!

'You're up early,' called Dick. 'And goodness me – are you going gardening or something? Why the spades?'

Martin looked sheepish and didn't seem to know what to say. Julian suddenly walked up to him and caught hold of his shoulder. 'Look here, Martin! There's some funny business going on here! What are you going to do with

those spades? Have you seen George? Do you know where she is, or anything about her? Come on, tell me!'

Martin shook his shoulder away from Julian's grip looking extremely surprised.

'George? No! What's happened to him?'

'George isn't a him – she's a her,' said Anne, still crying. 'She's disappeared. We thought she'd gone to the island to find her dog – and Timmy suddenly appeared at Kirrin Cottage, and brought us here!'

'So it looks as if George might be somewhere near here,'

said Julian. 'And I want to know if you've seen her or know anything of her whereabouts?'

'No, Julian. I swear I don't!' said Martin.

'Well, tell me what you're doing here so early in the morning, with spades,' said Julian, roughly. 'Who are you waiting for? Your father?'

'Yes,' said Martin.

'And what are you going to do?' asked Dick. 'Going exploring up the hole there?'

'Yes,' said Martin again, sullen and worried. 'No harm in that, is there?'

'It's all – very – queer!' said Julian, eyeing him and speaking slowly and loudly. 'But – let me tell you this – *we're* going exploring – not you! If there's anything queer up that hole, *we'll* find it! We shall not allow you or your father to get through the hole. So go and find him and tell him that!'

Martin didn't move. He went very white, and stared at Julian miserably. Anne went up to him, tears still on her face and put her hand on his arm.

'Martin, what is it? Why do you look like that? What's the mystery?'

And then, to the dismay and horror of everyone, Martin turned away with a noise that sounded very like a sob! He stood with his back to them, his shoulder shaking.

'Good gracious! What *is* up?' said Julian, in exasperation. 'Pull yourself together, Martin! Tell us what's worrying you.'

'Everything, everything!' said Martin, in a muffled voice. Then he swung round to face them. 'You don't know what it is to have no mother and no father – nobody who cares about you – and then . . .'

'But you *have* got a father!' said Dick at once.

'I haven't. He's not my father, that man. He's only my guardian, but he makes me call him father whenever we're on a job together.'

'A job? What sort of job?' said Julian.

'Oh any kind – all beastly,' said Martin. 'Snooping round and finding things out about people, and then getting money from them if we promise to say nothing – and receiving stolen goods and selling them – and helping people like the men who are after your uncle's secret . . .'

'*Oho!*' said Dick at once. 'Now we're coming to it. I *thought* you and Mr Curton were both suspiciously interested in Kirrin Island. What's this present job, then?'

'My guardian will half-kill me for telling all this,' said Martin. 'But, you see, they're planning to blow up the island – and it's about the worst thing I've ever been mixed up in – and I know your uncle is there – and perhaps George too now, you say. I can't go on with it!'

A few more tears ran down his cheeks. It was awful to see a boy crying like that, and the three felt sorry for Martin now. They were also full of horror when they heard him say that the island was to be blown up!

'How do you know this?' asked Julian.

'Well, Mr Curton's got a wireless receiver and transmitter as you know,' explained Martin, 'and so have the fellows on the island – the ones who are after your uncle's secret – so they can easily keep in touch with one another. They mean to get the secret if they can – if not they are going to blow the whole place sky-high so that *nobody* can get the secret. But they can't get away by boat because they don't know the way through those rocks . . .'

'Well, how will they get away then?' demanded Julian.

'We feel sure this hole that Timmy found the other day, leads down to the sea, and under the sea-bed to Kirrin Island,' said Martin. 'Yes, I know it sounds too mad to be true – but Mr Curton's got an old map which clearly shows there was once a passage under the sea-bed. If there is – well, the fellows across on the island can escape down it, after making all preparations for the island to be blown up. See?'

'Yes,' said Julian, taking a long breath. 'I *do* see. I see it all very clearly now. I see something else too! *Timmy* has found his way from the island, using that same passage you have just told us about – and *that's* why he's led us back here – to take us to the island and rescue Uncle Quentin and George.'

There was a deep silence. Martin stared at the ground. Dick and Julian thought hard. Anne sobbed a little. It all seemed quite unbelievable to her. Then Julian put his hand on Martin's arm.

'Martin! You did right to tell us. We may be able to prevent something dreadful. But you must help. We may need those spades of yours – and I expect you've got torches too. We haven't. We don't want to waste time going back and getting them – so will you come with us and help us? Will you lend us those spades and torches?'

'Would you trust me?' said Martin, in a low voice. 'Yes, I want to come and help you. And if we get in now, my guardian won't be able to follow, because he won't have a torch. We can get to the island and bring your uncle and George safely back.'

'Good for you!' said Dick. 'Well, come on then. We've been talking far too long. Come on down again, Ju. Hand him a spade and torch, Martin.'

'Anne you're not to come,' said Julian to his little sister. 'You're to go back and tell Aunt Fanny what's happened. Will you do that?'

'Yes. I don't want to come,' said Anne. 'I'll go back now. Do be careful, Julian!'

She climbed down with the boys and then stood and watched till all three had disappeared into the hole. Timmy, who had been waiting impatiently during the talking, barking now and again, was glad to find that at last they were going to make a move. He ran ahead in the tunnel, his eyes gleaming green every time he turned to see if they were following.

Anne began to climb up the steep side of the quarry again. Then, thinking she heard a cough, she stopped and crouched under a bush. She peered through the leaves and saw Mr Curton. Then she heard his voice.

'Martin! Where on earth are you?'

So he had come to look for Martin and go up the tunnel with him! Anne hardly dared to breathe. Mr Curton called again and again, then made an impatient noise and began to climb down the side of the quarry.

Suddenly he slipped! He clutched at a bush as he passed, but it gave way. He rolled quite near Anne, and caught sight of her. He looked astonished, but then his look became one of fear as he rolled more and more

quickly to the bottom of the deep quarry. Anne heard him give a deep groan as at last he came to a stop.

Anne peered down in fright. Mr Curton was sitting up, holding one of his legs and groaning. He looked up to see if he could spy Anne.

'Anne!' he called. 'I've broken my leg, I think. Can you fetch help? What are you doing here so early? Have you seen Martin?'

Anne did not answer. If he had broken his leg, then he couldn't go after the others! And Anne could get away quickly. She climbed carefully, afraid of rolling down to the bottom, and having to lie beside the horrid Mr Curton.

'Anne! Have you seen Martin? Look for him and get help for me, will you?' shouted Mr Curton, and then groaned again.

Anne climbed to the top of the quarry and looked down. She cupped her hands round her mouth and shouted loudly:

'You're a very wicked man. I shan't fetch help for you. I simply can't *bear* you!'

And, having got all that off her chest, the little girl shot off at top speed over the moor.

'I must tell Aunt Fanny. She'll know what to do! Oh I hope the others are safe. What shall we do if the island blows up? I'm glad, glad, glad I told Mr Curton he was a very wicked man.'

And on she ran, panting. Aunt Fanny would know what to do!

20

Everything boils up!

Meanwhile the three boys and Timmy were having a strange journey underground. Timmy led the way without faltering, stopping every now and again for the others to catch up with him.

The tunnel at first had a very low roof and the boys had to walk along in a stooping position, which was very tiring indeed. But after a bit the roof became higher and Julian, flashing his torch round, saw that the walls and floor, instead of being made of soil, were now made of rock. He tried to reckon out where they were.

'We've come practically straight towards the cliff,' he said to Dick. 'That's allowing for a few turns and twists. The tunnel has sloped down so steeply the last few hundred yards that I think we must be very far underground indeed.'

It was not until the boys heard the curious booming noise that George had heard in the caves, that they knew they must be under the rocky bed of the sea. They were walking under the sea to Kirrin Island. How strange, how unbelievably astonishing!

'It's like a peculiarly vivid dream,' said Julian. 'I'm not sure I like it very much! All right Tim – we're coming. Hallo – what's this?'

They all stopped. Julian flashed his torch ahead and saw a pile of fallen rocks. Timmy had managed to squeeze himself through a hole in them and go through to the other side, but the boys couldn't.

'This is where the spades come in, Martin!' said Dick, cheerfully. 'Take a hand!'

By dint of pushing and shovelling, the boys at last managed to move the pile of fallen rocks enough to make a way past. 'Thank goodness for the spades!' said Julian.

They went on, and were soon very glad of the spades again, to move another heap of rock. Timmy barked impatiently when they kept him waiting. He was very anxious to get back to George.

Soon they came to where the tunnel forked into two. But Timmy took the right-hand passage without hesitation, and when that one forked into three, he again chose one without stopping to think for a moment.

'Marvellous, isn't he?' said Julian. 'All done by smell! He's been this way once, so he knows it again. We should be completely lost under here if we came by ourselves.'

Martin was not enjoying this adventure at all. He said very little, but laboured on after the others. Dick guessed he was worrying about what was going to happen when the adventure was over. Poor Martin. All he wanted to do was to draw – and instead of that he had been dragged into one horrible job after another, and used as a cat's-paw by his evil guardian.

'Do you think we're anywhere near the island?' said Dick, at last. 'I'm getting tired of this!'

'Yes, we must be,' said Julian. 'In fact I think we'd

better be as quiet as we can, in case we come suddenly on the enemy!'

So, without speaking again, they went as quietly as they could – and then suddenly they saw a faint light ahead of them. Julian put out his hand to stop the others.

They were nearing the cave where George's father had his books and papers – where George had found him the night before. Timmy stood in front of them, listening too. He was not going to run headlong into danger!

They heard voices, and listened intently to see whose they were. 'George's – and Uncle Quentin's,' said Julian at last. And as if Timmy had also satisfied himself that those were indeed the two voices, the dog ran ahead and went into the lighted cave, barking joyfully.

'Timmy!' came George's voice, and they heard something overturn as she sprang up. 'Where have you been?'

'Woof,' said Timmy, trying to explain. 'Woof!'

And then Julian and Dick ran into the cave followed by Martin! Uncle Quentin and George stared in the very greatest amazement.

'Julian! Dick! And *Martin*! How did *you* get here?' cried George, while Timmy jumped and capered round her.

'I'll explain,' said Julian. 'It was Timmy that fetched us!' And he related the whole story of how Timmy had come into Kirrin Cottage in the early morning and had jumped on his bed, and all that had happened since.

And then, in their turn, Uncle Quentin and George told all that had happened to *them*!

'Where are the two men?' asked Julian.

'Somewhere on the island,' said George. 'I went scouting after them some time ago, and followed them up to where they get out into the little stone room. I think they're there until half past ten, when they'll go up and signal, so that people will think everything is all right.'

'Well, what are our plans?' said Julian. 'Will you come

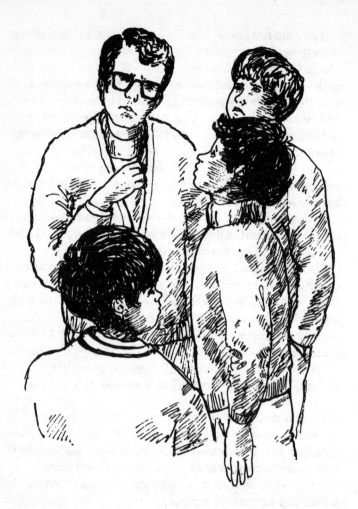

back down the passage under the sea with us? Or what shall we do?'

'Better not do that,' said Martin, quickly. 'My guardian may be coming – and he's in touch with other men. If he wonders where I am, and thinks something is up, he may call in two or three others, and we might meet them making their way up the passage.'

They did not know, of course, that Mr Curton was even then lying with a broken leg at the bottom of the quarry. Uncle Quentin considered.

'I've been given seven hours to say whether or not I will give the fellows my secret,' he said. 'That time will be up just after half past ten. Then the men will come down again to see me. I think between us we ought to be able to capture them – especially as we've got Timmy with us!'

'Yes – that's a good idea,' said Julian. 'We could hide somewhere till they come – and then set Timmy on them before they suspect anything!'

Almost before he had finished these words the light in the cave went out! Then a voice spoke out of the blackness.

'Keep still! One movement and I'll shoot.'

George gasped. What was happening? Had the men come back unexpectedly? Oh, why hadn't Timmy given them warning? She had been fondling his ears, so probably he had been unable to hear anything!

She held Timmy's collar, afraid that he would fly at the man in the darkness and be shot. The voice spoke again.

'Will you or will you not give us your secret?'

'Not,' said Uncle Quentin in a low voice.

'You will have this whole island, and all your work blown up then, and yourself too and the others?'

'Yes! You can do what you like!' suddenly yelled George. 'You'll be blown up yourself too. You'll never be able to get away in a boat – you'll go on the rocks!'

The man in the darkness laughed. 'We shall be safe,' he said. 'Now keep at the back of the cave. I have you covered with my revolver.'

They all crouched at the back. Timmy growled, but George made him stop at once. She did not know if the men knew he was free or not.

Quiet footsteps passed across the cave in the darkness. George listened, straining her ears. Two pairs of footsteps! Both men were passing through the cave. She knew where

145

they were going! They were going to escape by the under-sea passage – and leave the island to be blown up behind them!

As soon as the footsteps had died away, George switched on her torch. 'Father! Those men are escaping now, down the sea-tunnel. We must escape too – but not that way, My boat is on the shore. Let's get there quickly and get away before there's any explosion.'

'Yes, come along,' said her father. 'But if only I could get up into my tower, I could stop any wicked plan of theirs! They mean to use the power there. I know – but if I could get up to the glass room, I could undo all their plans!'

'Oh do be quick then, Father!' cried George, getting in quite a panic now. 'Save my island if you can!'

They all made their way through the cave up to the passage that led to the stone flight of steps from the little stone room. And there they had a shock!

The stone could not be opened from the inside! The men had altered the mechanism so that it could now only be opened from the outside.

In vain Uncle Quentin swung the lever to and fro. Nothing happened. The stone would not move.

'It's only from outside it can be opened,' he said in despair. 'We're trapped!'

They sat down on the stone steps in a row, one above the other. They were cold, hungry and miserable. What could they do now? Make their way back to the cave, and then go on down the under-sea tunnel?

'I don't want to do that,' said Uncle Quentin. 'I'm so afraid that if there is an explosion, it may crack the rocky bed of the sea, which is the roof of the tunnel – and then water would pour in. It wouldn't be pleasant if we happened to be there at that moment.'

'Oh no. Don't let's be trapped like that,' said George with a shudder. 'I couldn't bear it.'

146

'Perhaps I could get something to explode this stone away,' said her father, after a while. 'I've got plenty of stuff if only I've time to put it together.'

'Listen!' said Julian, suddenly. 'I can hear something outside this wall. Sh!'

They all listened intently. Timmy whined and scratched at the stone that would not move.

'It's voices!' cried Dick. 'Lots of them. Who can it be?'

'Be *quiet*,' said Julian, fiercely. 'We *must* find out!'

'I know, I know!' said George, suddenly. 'It's the fishermen who have come over in their boats! *That's* why the men didn't wait till half past ten! *That's* why they've gone in such a hurry! They saw the fisherboats coming!'

'Then Anne must have brought them!' cried Dick. 'She must have run home to Aunt Fanny, told her everything and given the news to the fishermen – and they've come to rescue us! Anne! ANNE! WE'RE HERE!'

Timmy began to bark deafeningly. The others encouraged him, because they felt certain that Timmy's bark was louder than their shouts!

'WOOF! WOOF! WOOF!'

Anne heard the barking and the shouting as soon as she ran into the little stone room. 'Where are you? Where are you?' she yelled.

'HERE! HERE! MOVE THE STONE!' yelled Julian, shouting so loudly that everyone near him jumped violently.

'Move aside, Miss – I can see which stone it is,' said a man's deep voice. It was one of the fishermen. He felt round and about the stone in the recess, sure it was the right one because it was cleaner than the others through being used as an entrance.

Suddenly he touched the right place, and found a tiny iron spike. He pulled it down – and the lever swung back behind it, and pulled the stone aside!

Everyone hurried out, one on top of the other! The six

fishermen standing in the little room stared in astonishment. Aunt Fanny was there too, and Anne. Aunt Fanny ran to her husband as soon as he appeared – but to her surprise he pushed her away quite roughly.

He ran out of the room, and hurried to the tower. Was he in time to save the island and everyone on it? Oh hurry, hurry!

The end of the adventure

'Where's he gone?' said Aunt Fanny, quite hurt. Nobody answered. Julian, George and Martin were watching the tower with anxious intensity. If only Uncle Quentin would appear at the top. Ah – there he was!

He had taken up with him a big stone. As everyone watched he smashed the glass round the tower with stone. Crash! Crash! Crash!

The wires that ran through the glass were broken and split as the glass crashed into pieces. No power could race through them now. Uncle Quentin leaned out of the broken glass room and shouted exultantly.

'It's all right! I was in time! I've destroyed the power that might have blown up the island – you're safe!'

George found that her knees were suddenly shaking. She had to sit down on the floor. Timmy came and licked her face wonderingly. Then he too sat down.

'What's he doing, smashing the tower up?' asked a burly fisherman. 'I don't understand all this.'

Uncle Quentin came down the tower and rejoined them. 'Another ten minutes and I should have been too late,' he said. 'Thank goodness, Anne, you all arrived when you did.'

'I ran all the way home, told Aunt Fanny, and we got the fishermen to come over as soon as they could get out their boats,' explained Anne. 'We couldn't think of any other way of rescuing you. Where are the wicked men?'

'Trying to escape down the under-sea tunnel,' said Julian. 'Oh – you don't know about that, Anne!' And he told her, while the fishermen listened open-mouthed.

'Look here,' said Uncle Quentin, when he had finished. 'As the boats are here, the men might as well take all my gear back with them. I've finished my job here. I shan't want the island any more.'

'Oh! Then *we* can have it!' said George, delighted. 'And there's plenty of the holidays left. We'll help to bring up what you want, Father.'

'We ought to get back as quickly as we can, so as to catch those fellows at the other end of the tunnel, sir,' said one of the fishermen.

'Yes. We ought,' said Aunt Fanny.

'Gracious! They'll find Mr Curton there with a broken leg,' said Anne, suddenly remembering.

The others looked at her in surprise. This was the first they had heard of Mr Curton being in the quarry. Anne explained.

'And I told him he was a very wicked man,' she ended triumphantly.

'Quite right,' said Uncle Quentin, with a laugh. 'Well, perhaps we'd better get my gear another time.'

'Oh, two of us can see to that for you now,' said the burly fisherman. 'Miss George here, she's got her boat in the cove, and you've got yours, sir. The others can go back with you, if you like – and Tom and me, we'll fix up your things and bring them across to the mainland later on. Save us coming over again, sir.'

'Right,' said Uncle Quentin, pleased. 'You do that then. It's down in the caves through that tunnel behind the stone.'

They all went down to the cove. It was a beautiful day and the sea was very calm, except just round the island where the waters were always rough. Soon the boats were being sailed or rowed to the mainland.

'The adventure is over!' said Anne. 'How queer – I didn't think it was one while it was happening – but now I see it was!'

'Another to add to our long list of adventures,' said Julian. 'Cheer up, Martin – don't look so blue. Whatever happens, we'll see you don't come out badly over this. You helped us, and you threw in your lot with us. We'll see that you don't suffer – won't we, Uncle Quentin? We'd never have got through those falls of rock if we hadn't had Martin and his spades!'

'Well – thanks,' said Martin. 'If you can get me away from my guardian – and never let me see him again – I'll be happy!'

'It's quite likely that Mr Curton will be put somewhere safe where he won't be able to see his friends for quite a long time,' said Uncle Quentin dryly. 'So I don't think you need worry.'

As soon as the boats reached shore, Julian, Dick, Timmy and Uncle Quentin went off to the quarry to see if Mr Curton was still there – and to wait for the other two men to come out of the tunnel!

Mr Curton was there all right, still groaning and calling for help. Uncle Quentin spoke to him sternly.

'We know your part in this matter, Curton. You will be dealt with by the police. They will be along in a short while.'

Timmy sniffed round Mr Curton, and then walked

151

away, nose in air, as if to say 'What a nasty bit of work!' The others arranged themselves at the mouth of the hole and waited.

But nobody came. An hour went by – two hours. Still nobody. 'I'm glad Martin and Anne didn't come,' said Uncle Quentin. 'I do wish we'd brought sandwiches.'

At that moment the police arrived, scrambling down the steep sides of the quarry. The police doctor was with them and he saw to Mr Curton's leg. Then, with the help of the others, he got the man to the top with great difficulty.

'Julian, go back and get sandwiches,' said Uncle Quentin at last. 'It looks as if we've got a long wait!'

Julian went back, and was soon down the quarry with neat packets of ham sandwiches and a thermos of hot coffee. The two policemen who were still left offered to stay and watch, if Uncle Quentin wanted to go home.

'Dear me, no!' he said. 'I want to see the faces of these two fellows when they come out. It's going to be one of the nicest moments of my life! The island is not blown up. My secret is safe. My book is safe. My work is finished. And I just want to tell these things to my two dear friends!'

'You know, Father, I believe they've lost their way underground,' said George. 'Julian said there were many different passages. Timmy took the boys through the right ones, of course – but they would have been quite lost if they hadn't had him with them!'

Her father's face fell at the thought of the men being lost underground. He did so badly want to see their dismayed faces when they arrived in the quarry!

'We could send Timmy in,' said Julian. 'He would soon find them and bring them out. Wouldn't you, Tim?'

'Woof,' said Timmy, agreeing.

'Oh yes – that's a good idea,' said George. 'They won't hurt him if they think he can show them the way out! Go in in, Timmy. Find them boy; find them! Bring them here!'

'Woof,' said Timmy, obligingly, and disappeared under the shelf of rock.

Everyone waited, munching sandwiches and sipping coffee. And then they heard Timmy's bark again, from underground!

There was a panting noise, then a scraping sound as

somebody came wriggling out from under the rock. He stood up – and then he saw the silent group watching him. He gasped.

'Good morning, Johnson,' said Uncle Quentin, in an amiable voice. 'How are you?'

Johnson went white. He sat down on the nearby heather. 'You win!' he said.

'I do,' said Uncle Quentin. 'In fact, I win handsomely. Your little plan went wrong. My secret is still safe – and next year it will be given to the whole world!'

There was another scraping sound and the second man arrived. He stood up too – and then he saw the quietly watching group.

'Good morning, Peters,' said Uncle Quentin. 'So nice to see you again. How did you like your underground walk? We found it better to come by sea.'

Peters looked at Johnson, and he too sat down suddenly. 'What's happened?' he said to Johnson.

'It's all up,' said Johnson. Then Timmy appeared, wagging his tail, and went to George.

'I bet they were glad when Timmy came up to them!' said Julian.

Johnson looked at him. 'Yes. We were lost in those hateful tunnels. Curton said he'd come to meet us, but he never came.'

'No. He's probably in the prison hospital by now, with a broken leg,' said Uncle Quentin. 'Well, constable – do your duty.'

Both men were at once arrested. Then the whole company made their way back over the moor. The two men were put into a police car and driven off. The rest of the company went into Kirrin Cottage to have a good meal.

'I'm most terribly hungry,' said George. 'Joanna, have you got anything nice for breakfast?'

'Not much,' said Joanna, from the kitchen. 'Only bacon and eggs and mushrooms!'

154

'Ooooh!' said Anne, 'Joanna, you shall have the OBCBE!'

'And what may that be?' cried Joanna, but Anne couldn't remember.

'It's a decoration!' she cried.

'Well, I'm not a Christmas tree!' shouted back Joanna. 'You come and help with the breakfast!'

It was a very jolly breakfast that the seven of them – no eight, for Timmy must certainly be counted – sat down to. Martin, now that he was free of his guardian, became quite a different boy.

The children made plans for him. 'You can stay with the coastguard, because he likes you – he kept on and on saying you weren't a bad boy! And you can come and play with us and go to the island. And Uncle Quentin will see if he can get you into an art-school. He says you deserve a reward for helping to save his wonderful secret!'

Martin glowed with pleasure. It seemed as if a load had fallen away from his shoulders. 'I've never had a chance till now,' he said, 'I'll make good. You see if I don't!'

'Mother! Can we go and stay on Kirrin Island and watch the tower being taken down tomorrow?' begged George. 'Do say yes! And can we stay there a whole week? We can sleep in that little room as we did before.'

'Well – I suppose you can!' said her mother, smiling at George's eager face. 'I'd rather like to have your father to myself for a few days and feed him up a bit.'

'Oh – that reminds me, Fanny,' said her husband, suddenly. 'I tried some soup you left for me, the night before last. And my dear, it was horrible! Quite bad!'

'Oh *Quentin*! I told you to pour it away! You know I did,' said his wife, distressed. 'It must have been completely bad. You really are dreadful.'

They all finished their breakfast at last, and went out into the garden. They looked across Kirrin Bay to Kirrin Island. It looked lovely in the morning sun.

'We've had a lot of adventures together,' said Julian. 'More than most children. They *have* been exciting, haven't they?'

Yes – they have, but now we must say good-bye to the Five, and to Kirrin Island too. Good-bye, Julian, Dick, George, Anne – and Timmy. But only Timmy hears our good-bye, for he has such sharp ears.

FAMOUS FIVE SERIES